I0752658

THE PLACE WE BELONG

Carolyn Hinds

Published by Innovo Publishing, LLC
www.innovopublishing.com
1-888-546-2111

Innovo Publishing LLC is a Christ-centered publisher located near Memphis, TN. Since 2008, Innovo has published quality books, eBooks, audiobooks, music, screenplays, and online and physical curricula that support the Great Commission, equip believers, and help create a positive Christian worldview. Innovo's capabilities and global reach provide Christian authors, artists, and ministries access to the world for Christ. To learn more about Innovo Publishing, visit our website at innovopublishing.com. To connect with other Christian creatives and to learn best practices for creating, publishing, marketing, and selling Christian titles, visit the Christian Publishing Portal at cpportal.com.

The Place We Belong

Library of Congress Control Number: 2026905066
ISBN: 979-8-88928-165-8

Cover Design & Interior Layout: Innovo Publishing, LLC

Printed in the United States of America
U.S. Printing History
First Edition: 2026

To my husband, Marco: my home, my place of belonging, and my steady anchor and safe harbor.

To my best friend, Brenda: my "Liz," whose friendship reflects the steadfast love of Christ and whose life is a daily example of faith lived well.

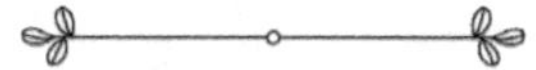

Chapter 1

THE SILENCE AFTER

Grace cradled the chipped mug of coffee in both hands, letting the warmth press into her fingers. It was too early, too quiet, and far too loud all at once.

Michael's chair sat empty across from her at the kitchen table. His Bible still rested on the corner, a slip of paper marking the last passage he read aloud to her: "Though the mountains be shaken and the hills be removed, yet my unfailing love for you will not be shaken"—*Isaiah something.* She couldn't remember the verse number today.

The kitchen had once been a place of noise—laughter, arguments over toast, hockey game recaps. Now the only sounds were the tick of the wall clock and the distant bark of a dog that wasn't hers.

People had come. For two weeks, the phone rang. Her freezer overflowed with casseroles, and church friends stopped by with pie and hugs. Then, as suddenly as they came, they were gone. Life moved on. For everyone but her.

She looked out the window. Morning mist clung to the lawn like a prayer unfinished. She whispered aloud, "God, I don't know what I'm still doing here."

No answer. Not yet. Just the hum of the fridge and the ache in her chest.

She reached for the radio and turned it on—habit. The voice of a singer she didn't recognize filled the room: "Come what may . . . I know You're good, I know You're kind."

The song pierced something inside her. She closed her eyes.

Maybe it wasn't about answers. Maybe it was about listening.

Maybe it was time to leave.

* * *

The coffee had gone cold. Grace poured the rest into the sink and washed the mug, taking far too long to dry it. Every movement in the kitchen felt deliberate now, like she was choreographing her own presence, proving she still existed.

She wandered into the living room, where the sunlight fell across the photo wall: birthdays, camping trips, weddings, Christmases. She stared at one picture—Michael in his flannel jacket, standing next to her by the firepit. She couldn't recall who had taken it. She couldn't remember when. He had his arm around her, and she was laughing.

"You always knew who I was," she whispered to the photo. "Even when I didn't."

The ache swelled in her chest again—loneliness, grief, and something else. Something quieter, more insistent. Emptiness.

She sat on the edge of the couch and picked up her old journal from the coffee table. The leather cover was worn, the pages soft from years of flipping. She paged through prayers written in ink and in tears. Somewhere near the middle, her handwriting grew shaky—dated just after Michael's diagnosis. Then . . . *silence.*

A new page stared back at her. She lightly tapped her pen against the margin, hesitated, then wrote:

God . . . I don't know who I am anymore.

She stopped and stared at the words. There it was. The truth.

The radio was still playing softly in the kitchen. A new voice filled the room—familiar, almost too familiar:

You tell me I'm enough when I can't see
the light.

Grace froze. That song always broke her wide open.

You lift me up in strength when I'm losing
the fight.

She laid the pen down, closed her eyes, and let the lyrics wash over her. The tears came silently. She didn't wipe them away. "I don't feel any of that right now," she said aloud. "But I want to."

The truth in the words reached something deep in her—a longing she hadn't named. Not just to survive this loss, but to *live.* To know she still mattered. To believe that God still saw her, had something for her. That she could belong again, somewhere.

She looked back at the journal and whispered, "What if there's still more?"

That's when the idea came—not loud or dramatic, but quiet. Just a sense, a pull, like the tide easing in without fanfare.

She didn't need all the answers. Just the first step.

Later that afternoon, Grace pulled the suitcase down from the closet shelf. She hadn't used it since their anniversary trip to Prince Edward Island.

She smiled faintly, then wiped the handle clean and set it by the bed. One step at a time.

She didn't know exactly where she was going. But for the first time in weeks, she had somewhere to go.

The next morning, Grace sat on the edge of her bed, her phone in hand, thumb hovering over a familiar contact:

Liz - Bestie ♥

She hadn't told her about the packing yet. About the restlessness. About the quiet that had turned from sacred to suffocating.

She tapped *Call.*

"Grace!" Liz answered immediately, her voice a balm. "I was just thinking of you."

Grace swallowed the lump in her throat. "You always say that."

"Because it's always true," Liz replied, gentle now. "How are you really?"

Grace hesitated, then exhaled. "I think I need to leave for a bit. Not forever. Just . . . I can't stay here right now. I feel like I've disappeared."

The line was quiet, but not with distance. Liz knew when to wait.

"I thought maybe, if it's not a terrible time, I could come down east. Not right to your house," Grace added quickly. "Just rent something nearby. For a month or two. Catch my breath. Find my feet again."

"Oh, Gracie," Liz said, and Grace heard the smile. "I've been praying you'd say that. You don't need to explain. Just come. The pace out here is good for the soul. I'll help you find a spot near the river. We'll drink too much tea and figure the rest out."

For the first time in weeks, Grace felt a flicker of something like hope.

"Okay," she whispered. "I'm coming."

Grace wrote her first journal entry since Michael's death:

It's strange how empty a full life can feel once it's been turned upside down.

I used to know who I was. Wife. Friend. Hostess. Helper. Now I just know I miss him, and I don't recognize this house without him in it.

Maybe it's not about going back to what was. Maybe it's about going forward to find out who I am now.

I hope there's still something in me worth discovering.

Chapter 2

A SEAT AT THE COUNTER

Grace's hands relaxed on the steering wheel for the first time in hours on her second day of travel, as she coasted into the quiet main street of Harbor's End. She hadn't planned to stop here—hadn't planned much of anything, really. But something about the way the road curved into town, revealing a cluster of old buildings with hand-painted signs and tidy porches, had nudged her off the highway.

A hanging sign swung gently in the breeze:

Maggie's Diner
Home-Cooked Since 1974

Perfect.

She parked under the shade of a maple tree, stepped out, and stretched. The salty air hit her first—clean, honest, comforting. It reminded her of childhood summers by the lake with her mother's homemade bread and sun-warmed sheets.

The diner door jingled as she stepped inside. Chrome-edged stools lined the counter, and booths with red leather seats stretched along the windows. It was the kind of place time had forgotten, and Grace was grateful for that.

Only a few patrons were scattered around—two older men nursing coffees near the back and a woman flipping through a paperback at the window booth. Behind the counter stood a sturdy woman with short, silver hair, a tired but kind expression, and flour dust on her black apron. She glanced up from wiping the counter.

"Sit wherever you like, hon," she said, her voice warm and scratchy, like a well-loved quilt.

Grace offered a small smile and slid onto a counter stool. "I'll take one of those grilled cheese specials I saw on the sign. And a tea, if you've got it."

"We've always got tea," the woman replied with a wink. "I'm Maggie."

"Grace," she answered, feeling oddly comforted by the simplicity of the exchange.

As Maggie poured hot water over a teabag and slid the sandwich onto the griddle, the door flew open, and a gust of chatter followed.

"Oh, Lord help us," Maggie muttered, eyes widening.

A bus had pulled up outside—its side marked with a retirement village logo. A dozen seniors were already filtering in, some with canes, others in pairs, all of them looking hungry and cheerful.

Maggie turned to Grace, her eyes apologetic. "Driver must've missed the highway turnoff. Happens once in a while, but I usually get a heads-up."

She moved into action, flipping sandwiches, grabbing cups. A teenage girl in a hoodie emerged from the back, drying her hands on a towel and eyeing the crowd like a deer in headlights.

Grace slid off her stool and stepped around the counter. "Need a hand?" she asked.

Maggie hesitated for half a second.

"You ever slung plates before?"

"High school. I was good at it."

Maggie grinned. "Well, let's find out if it's like riding a bike."

Within minutes, Grace was refilling coffee cups, delivering soup bowls, and remembering how to carry three plates at once without disaster. The noise swelled around her—laughter, questions, the clink of cutlery—and she didn't feel overwhelmed. She felt alive.

The bus rolled away with a cheerful honk, leaving behind a scattering of crumbs, emptied mugs, and the scent of warm butter. Grace stood at the sink, sleeves rolled up, hands immersed in suds. Maggie was wiping down tables in slow, deliberate circles.

"You sure you're not here for a job interview?" Maggie called over her shoulder.

Grace laughed. "Nope. Just lunch."

"Well, you've earned a piece of pie, at the very least."

They reconvened at the counter, the hum of the kitchen now replaced with the occasional creak of the building settling and the quiet rattle of spoons in mismatched teacups. Maggie poured Grace a fresh cup of tea, slid a plate of apple pie between them, and joined her at the counter—elbows propped, back slightly slouched.

"Thanks for helping. Most would've just watched and shaken their heads."

"I figured I could either help or get steamrolled by a crowd of hungry seniors."

Maggie snorted. "A force to be reckoned with, for sure."

They sat in companionable silence for a few sips. The clatter of lunchtime faded into a late afternoon lull. Grace caught Maggie studying her face.

"You're not just passing through, are you?" Maggie asked gently.

Grace hesitated. "I'm not sure yet. I didn't plan to stop here at all. But the diner felt . . . safe."

Maggie nodded slowly. "You've got the eyes of someone who's been through something."

Grace looked down at her cup. "My husband died a year ago. I kept waiting for the fog to lift, for life to pick up again. But after the casseroles stopped coming and people went back to their own lives, I realized I didn't have much of one myself."

Maggie rested her hand lightly on Grace's. "I lost my Henry five years ago. Diner's kept me upright. That and my boy—well, man now—he helps when I holler loud enough."

"Does it get easier?" Grace asked, voice barely above a whisper.

Maggie gave a half-smile. "It gets different. Softer around the edges. You stop expecting him to walk through the door, but you still hear his voice in your head when you burn the bacon."

They shared a quiet laugh. Grace felt a warmth she hadn't in months—something like kinship. Maggie sipped her tea, then tilted her head thoughtfully.

"You know, I might have a solution to that 'not sure where to go' look you've got."

Grace raised an eyebrow.

"A friend of mine just moved into a retirement place. She hasn't been able to sell her old house yet. Cute little place—bit creaky, but it's got character. I think she'd be open to renting it out short term, especially to someone who isn't going to throw wild parties."

"Sounds ideal," Grace said, a wry smile playing on her lips.

"I can call her. Get you a key. Even if just for a month or two. Give you time to breathe."

Grace blinked back a sudden sting in her eyes. She hadn't expected kindness today. Not from a stranger. Not from anyone, really.

"That would be . . . wonderful. Thank you."

Maggie stood and gave her a wink. "Sometimes the road brings us where we need to be before we even know we're looking."

Grace looked around the diner—its faded menus, the humming fridge, the corner booth where two teenagers had just come in for milkshakes—and she realized she had stopped thinking about where she'd been and started wondering where she might go next.

That night, she called Liz to let her know that her arrival would be delayed. For how long, she couldn't be sure, but she knew she had stumbled on something worth pressing into, at least for a bit. Liz, in her supportive way, listened to Grace recount the day's events and said that she would plan to come up for a visit once she was settled in.

Grace curled up on the bed in her motel room and opened her journal.

The road out of home wasn't just paved in asphalt—it was paved in fear, uncertainty, and just enough courage to hit the gas. But there was also something waiting for me on the other end: stillness. Possibility.

A woman in a diner who reminded me that even tired hearts have something left to give. Maybe leaving wasn't running away. Maybe it was the beginning of running toward something.

Chapter 3

UNFOLDING

The house Maggie helped her find was a small, storybook bungalow tucked behind a white picket fence in need of repainting. The porch sagged a little on one side, and the garden had gone wild—but Grace loved it. There was something freeing about having no expectations here. Just a clean slate and time to figure out what came next.

She spent the first few days wandering the sleepy streets of Harbor's End, noting the places she'd return to—a gift shop with wind chimes in the window, the post office wrapped in faded brick, the church with peeling white paint and a crooked bell tower. Everything moved slower here. She exhaled more deeply than she had in months.

On the third day, she stepped back into Maggie's Diner just before the lunch lull.

"Back already?" Maggie asked from the kitchen pass-through, a smirk in her voice.

Grace grinned. "I was hoping for another slice of that pie."

Maggie wiped her hands on her apron and came around the counter. "You're in luck. Apple crumble's fresh from the oven." She paused, then added, "I've been meaning to ask—you interested in helping out here a little more officially?"

Grace blinked. "Like . . . on the schedule?"

"I'm not talking full time. Just afternoons. Give me a chance to go home, put my feet up before the dinner crowd. We keep it simple: grilled cheese, soups, meatloaf if it's Thursday. I've got a high school kid, Mina, doing kitchen prep and helping out around here, but she's heading off to college in a few weeks. I just need someone steady with a good attitude."

Grace felt something lift in her chest. A job offer wasn't just about the work; it was about being seen. Needed.

"I'd love to," she said, surprising herself with how quickly she meant it.

"Good," Maggie said. "You already passed the senior bus rush test. If you can handle them, you can handle anything."

By the following week, Grace had fallen into a rhythm—mornings puttering around, afternoons at the diner, evenings in the little house with her feet tucked under a quilt and a mug of peppermint tea by her side. She still felt the ache of loss, but it was less sharp here. More like a low hum she carried with her.

One Thursday afternoon, as she was wiping the counter and humming softly to herself, she heard the bell over the door ring.

Jonas Reid.

He was a tall, weathered man in his sixties, maybe early seventies, broad-shouldered and quiet. He came in every morning at 8 a.m. sharp, ordered a black coffee and toast, sat in the same corner booth, and left exactly twenty-five minutes later. Then again in the afternoon, usually around 2:15, for a refill and a glance through the local paper.

Grace had served him several times now, and while he always offered a polite nod or a brief thank-you, they'd never exchanged more than ten words. But today, something was different.

She hadn't realized she was singing aloud, just softly—"You Say" by Lauren Daigle, a song she often whispered under her breath when the sadness crept up.

Jonas paused mid-step, tilted his head. "That's a good song."

Grace turned, caught slightly off guard. "Oh, sorry, I didn't realize I was singing out loud."

"Don't apologize," he said, settling into his booth. "It's rare to hear something real these days."

She brought his coffee over, curiosity stirring. "You know it?"

He nodded, eyes still on the cup. "My granddaughter sent it to me a couple years back. Said it reminded her of her mom . . . my daughter. We lost her a while ago."

The silence that followed wasn't uncomfortable. It felt like reverence—like the space between pain and connection.

"I'm sorry," Grace said quietly. "I lost my husband last year."

Jonas looked up at her then. Really looked. "Then you understand."

Grace folded her cloth and leaned lightly against the counter. "Some days. Others, I just breathe and hope it's enough."

Jonas gave a slow, thoughtful nod. "That's more faith than most people realize."

They sat in the silence again, not because there was nothing to say, but because something unspoken had been shared.

⁂

Later that afternoon, Grace was refilling the sugar jars when a blur of backpack and dark curls burst through the side door.

"Sorry, Maggie!" the girl called out, breathless. "Wi-Fi dropped again during my economics class."

"You're good," Maggie said from the back, without turning. "Homework first, then chopping onions."

The girl slid behind the counter, earbuds still half-hanging from her collar. She caught sight of Grace and smiled shyly.

"You're the new help?" she asked, popping a piece of gum in her mouth.

Grace smiled back. "Something like that. You must be Mina."

"Yep. Senior in high school. Doing my first college course online too."

"Economics, huh?"

Mina groaned. "It's the worst. Just tell me what to memorize; don't make me explain trade policy like I'm Carney or something."

Grace laughed. "Well, you're not alone in thinking that. I once dropped out of a marketing course because I couldn't figure out what the professor was saying—and he spoke English."

Mina brightened. "That actually makes me feel better."

"Good. Everyone deserves to feel like they're not alone."

The words settled over them quietly. Mina tucked a stray curl behind her ear and nodded.

Grace noticed the tension in her shoulders, the guarded edge in her voice. She saw something of her younger self in Mina—a girl trying hard to hold it together, to move forward without letting anyone see the cracks.

I didn't expect the rhythm of this town to feel so right.

Maggie's offer was simple: lend a hand. But the gift was far greater.

Purpose feels like the first breath after holding it for too long. And then there was the man who sat alone, and the girl who chopped vegetables like music.

Maybe God's way of stitching us together is letting our stories overlap just enough to heal the frayed edges.

Chapter 4

LEARNING TO WALK AGAIN

The fog rolled in early that morning, hugging the edges of the house like a shawl. Grace sat by the front window with a steaming cup of coffee, wrapped in a worn cardigan that still faintly smelled of lavender and lemon from home. The quiet was more than stillness; it was peace. It had been a long time since she'd felt anything close to that.

She opened her journal, the one Liz had given her years ago. The cover read *Still, I Will Rise* in delicate script. A verse from Isaiah was written on the inside cover in Liz's handwriting:

> *When you pass through the waters, I will be with you.*

Grace had underlined it a dozen times since.

Today feels different. I can't explain why, but it does. Maybe it's the way the light came through the fog this morning. Maybe it's the rhythm I'm settling into. Or maybe it's just hope, finally stretching its legs.

By late morning, the fog had lifted and the town began to stir. The bells above the diner door jingled as Grace pushed it open. She was early, but Maggie was already behind the counter pouring coffee for one of the town's older regulars.

"Morning," Maggie called. "You're a sight for sore eyes."

Grace laughed. "You say that like it's been a busy morning."

"It has," Maggie said frankly. "I'm glad you're early."

Mina was already in the kitchen, earbuds in and head bobbing as she chopped vegetables with surprising efficiency.

"I think I'm learning how this place works," Grace said, grabbing an apron from the hook. "Rhythmic chaos."

"Just wait till the supper rush," Maggie said, already halfway out the door. "Back at three. Try not to burn the place down."

The lunch rush was steady but manageable. Mina handled the grill, Grace handled the people, and by 2:30 the diner had emptied out. The last to linger was Jonas Reid, quietly sipping his coffee by the window. Grace refilled his mug and, without asking, slid into the seat across from him.

He looked surprised but not displeased.

"Don't usually see you sitting."

"I don't usually see you talking."

He chuckled softly, stirring his coffee without adding anything to it.

"Fair enough," he said. "But today's different."

Grace nodded. "It is."

They sat in silence for a moment. Grace looked out at the street—so still, like the town itself was holding its breath.

"When Michael died," she began, "I thought I'd stop breathing too. People came around. They were kind. But it was like watching someone help you fix a house while the foundation was still crumbling beneath you."

Jonas studied her face, thoughtful. "Everyone expects grief to have a timetable. A six-month expiration date."

"Yes," she whispered. "Exactly that."

"I lost my daughter six years ago."

Grace looked up.

"She was twenty-three. Drunk driver."

"I'm so sorry, Jonas."

He nodded, eyes on the coffee. "After she died, I stopped going to church. Stopped answering phone calls. I didn't stop believing, I just . . . didn't want to talk to Him anymore."

Grace swallowed hard. "I know that silence. That ache where prayer used to live."

"But I also knew," Jonas said slowly, "that He hadn't left me. I was just too wounded to walk. And eventually, I realized faith doesn't mean always walking strong. Sometimes it's just choosing to stand when you'd rather curl up in the dark."

Grace blinked, fighting the sudden heat in her eyes. "Some days I still feel like I'm standing in deep water. Like the ground's not solid and the tide's about to pull me under."

He nodded again. "But you're still standing."

She smiled faintly. "Barely."

"That still counts."

She let the silence settle again, then asked, "Do you think God brings us into the deep places just so we'll learn to trust Him more?"

"I think He meets us there. And teaches us to walk again, even when our legs shake."

Grace looked at him, something soft opening in her chest. It wasn't romantic; it was holy. "I guess God is never really done with any of us. But it is up to us to keep taking that next step. I'm glad you spoke today."

"I'm glad you sang yesterday."

Her eyebrows lifted, and she smiled.

He gave a small smile. "I heard it. And I think God did too."

Grace walked home slowly, the sun dipping low behind the trees. The wind carried the scent of salt and pine. Her legs ached, but it was the good kind of tired. Her soul felt steadier, like the shaking had quieted a little.

I didn't think I had anything to offer. Not to this town. Not to God. Not even to myself. But today reminded me that showing up is sometimes enough. That healing is often slow. And that God—He meets us in the deep to teach us how to trust again.

Today, I learned to walk a little.

Chapter 5

A GENTLE UNFOLDING

The air had a crispness the next morning that hinted at early fall. Grace stepped out onto the porch with her coffee, watching the sunrise soften the sky in strokes of peach and gold. The scent of woodsmoke curled faintly in the air, and for the first time since arriving, she found herself smiling without effort.

She returned to the diner just after nine, apron in hand, and was greeted by Maggie with a wave and a knowing look. Grace had become part of the rhythm now, not just filling a role but becoming one of the faces people expected to see.

Jonas came in early too, quieter than usual. He lingered over his coffee, watching the steam rise and twist like thoughts too heavy to speak aloud. Grace noticed him glance toward the counter more than once, as if debating something. As he finally stood and walked toward the door, he paused beside the counter and spoke just above a whisper. "Thanks again . . . for yesterday."

Grace smiled gently. "I'm glad we talked. I meant what I said—God isn't finished with either of us yet."

Jonas gave a thoughtful nod. "Thanks for the reminder."

She touched his arm briefly. "That's God's doing. I'm just learning to listen again."

He gave a short, quiet chuckle. "Well, I think He's using you, whether you know it or not."

She understood. Some moments echo longer than others.

***

Early that afternoon, as Mina prepped quietly in the back, Grace found herself wondering what lay ahead for this young woman. Before the lunch rush, she had slipped a small leather-bound notebook into her bag—a simple gift for the end of the day. It was Mina's last shift before heading off to school.

Grace grabbed a rag and began to wipe down tables, taking stock of the small moments: an elderly couple sharing soup, a toddler banging a spoon against the table, someone humming near the register. This, she thought, was what it meant to belong somewhere.

Then the bell jingled, and in walked a man she hadn't seen before. Late forties. Rugged. Eyes that scanned the room like they didn't quite trust it yet. Maggie looked up from her book behind the counter and called out, "Glenn, you're late."

He grunted in reply and made his way to the coffee pot, pouring himself a cup without asking.

Grace raised an eyebrow. "Help yourself."

He glanced at her. "Family discount."

Maggie chuckled. "My son. Don't mind him. He growls more than he bites."

Grace studied him. There was something shuttered in his expression, something locked up tight.

"Grace," she said, offering a hand.

She noticed his hesitation—not just in his hand but in his eyes. There was weariness there, more than physical. Grace didn't push, just waited, steady and open. She had learned recently that people opened up when you didn't try to pry them loose.

He hesitated, then shook it. "Glenn."

Their hands met briefly, and Grace felt the cold of someone still living behind walls. But she didn't pull away. She just smiled.

Later, when Maggie left for the day, she gave Grace a nod. "You're good for this place," she said. "And maybe for some of the people in it too."

Grace finished her shift and walked home as the evening settled in, full of questions but also something new: a quiet assurance that maybe she was in the right place, at exactly the right time.

I thought healing would come in solitude, but maybe it's actually found in the middle of small-town noise and complicated people.

Glenn doesn't know it yet, but something about him feels familiar. Maybe broken recognizes broken. Maybe hope does too.

Today, I felt the quiet beginning of something new.

Chapter 6

SHIFTING GROUND

Grace had just set down the mop bucket when the diner door creaked open. She looked up, expecting the mail carrier. It was Jonas.

"You're early," she said with a smile.

"Didn't sleep," he said simply, sliding onto his usual booth.

Grace nodded and poured him a fresh cup. "Want to talk about it?"

He didn't answer right away. Instead, he watched the steam rise from the mug. He followed the twisting lines of steam, watching them rise and dissolve, the way his own thoughts tangled and disappeared before he could give them shape. Finally, he said, "I've been thinking about what you said. About God not being finished with me."

She leaned on the counter. "And?"

"I want to believe it's true," he said, voice low. "But part of me wonders if I've just . . . missed too much. Wasted too many years in this . . . bitterness."

Grace considered her reply. "Jonas, do you remember Peter? How he denied Jesus three times, after walking beside Him for years?"

He nodded.

"Jesus didn't shame him. He met him where he was—on the shore, with breakfast and forgiveness. That's the kind of God we have. Not one who scolds, but one who restores. He used fishermen and tax collectors and a shepherd boy with a slingshot. He chooses the ones the world overlooks. The underdogs, the weary, the ones who think it's too late. That's who He builds His kingdom with."

Jonas looked at her, eyes a little glassy. "And you believe He could still do that for me?"

"I do. And more importantly—*He* does."

Just then, the door jingled again. Glenn stepped inside, took one glance at the scene, and headed for the corner booth.

Grace gave him a nod, and he returned it with a grunt. *Baby steps*, she thought.

⁂

The afternoon was quiet. Grace noticed Glenn writing something in a small notepad while he drank his coffee. She brought over a slice of pie—on the house.

"I didn't ask for this," he said without looking up.

"Consider it a peace offering," she said.

He sighed. "You don't have to try so hard, you know. I'm not exactly good company."

"I'm not looking for good company," Grace replied. "I'm looking for honest company."

That made him pause.

She nodded to the notepad. "What are you working on?"

He quickly closed it. "Just doodling."

She didn't press, just gave a small smile and walked away.

···

That night, Grace sat on her porch with a blanket over her knees and the stars overhead. For a long time after Michael's death, nights like this had been unbearable—too quiet, too vast. She had sat in the same chair, staring at the same stars, wondering if her life had ended alongside his. But somewhere along the way, the silence had shifted. What once mocked her loneliness had become space for God to whisper that she was not forgotten. A breeze danced through the trees, whispering secrets only God could fully understand.

I'm learning that healing isn't loud. Sometimes it's a quiet conversation over coffee. A nod from someone who never nods. A notepad half-hidden.

Faith doesn't always return with fanfare. Sometimes it tiptoes back in the form of presence. Today, it came with a pie and a whisper of hope.

Chapter 7

THE EDGE OF SOMETHING

The afternoon sunlight filtered through the front windows of the diner, scattering soft gold across the booths. Grace stood at the counter, wiping down a tray while watching a pair of children press their noses against the glass of the pastry case.

Jonas sat in his usual spot near the window, a notebook open beside his coffee cup. He wasn't writing, just staring down at the blank page like it might blink first.

"You ever actually write anything in there?" Grace asked, walking over with the coffee pot.

Jonas smirked and slid the notebook toward her. "Empty pages don't judge."

"Maybe not," she said, topping off his mug. "But they don't tell your story either."

He chuckled low in his throat. "You always have to do that?"

"Do what?"

"Shine light into places people are trying to keep dim?"

Grace leaned against the edge of the table. "You sat by the window, Jonas. I'm just the one offering the view."

That made him laugh out loud—a warm, surprised sound that turned a few heads. Even Glenn's.

He'd just walked in, hands in his jacket pockets, and paused by the door. He looked at Jonas, then at Grace, then made his way to his usual booth in the corner, eyes lowered.

Later that day, Maggie had taken off early for a hair appointment in the next town over, leaving Grace to manage the floor. The diner was quiet enough that Grace slipped Jonas a slice of pie and joined him again.

He took a bite, then pointed at the notebook. "I've been thinking about your Peter story."

Grace raised an eyebrow. "Yeah?"

"You said Jesus didn't shame him. That He restored him."

"I believe that."

Jonas nodded. "I've felt shame for a long time. For being bitter. For checking out. For letting the pain be louder than my faith."

Grace reached over and gently tapped the notebook. "That pain? It's part of your testimony. And testimonies don't help anyone if they stay hidden."

He didn't speak for a moment. Then, softly, "You really think God still wants to use someone like me?"

She looked him straight in the eyes. "Jonas, God used a man who ran away from Nineveh, a woman who hid spies on her rooftop, a stuttering shepherd to speak before kings. You think He's done with you? No chance."

Something shifted in Jonas then. Not a full change—but a spark. A softening.

"I'm scared," he admitted.

Grace smiled. "Good. So was Peter when he stepped out onto the water. But he walked anyway."

⁂

From across the room, Glenn watched the exchange. He didn't mean to eavesdrop—at least, not consciously—but something about the way Grace spoke stirred something long dormant in him.

He'd once believed in second chances too. Before everything fell apart. Before trust became a luxury he couldn't afford.

As Grace returned to wiping the counter, Glenn stood, walking up with his empty cup.

"Need a refill?" she asked.

He handed over the mug. "What's his story?"

Grace glanced over at Jonas, then back at Glenn. "You could ask him."

Glenn snorted. "Not really my style."

"No," she agreed, pouring fresh coffee. "You'd rather listen from a distance."

He gave her a flat look. "You think you've got me figured out?"

"Nope," she said, handing him the cup. "But I think you've got more to say than you let on."

Glenn hesitated, then offered a dry half-smile. "You ever get tired of digging into people?"

"All the time," she said with a grin. "But sometimes . . . I'm pleasantly surprised."

⁂

That night, Grace walked home beneath a sky streaked with fading lavender. The air was cooler now—the early September summer quietly bowing to late September fall.

She stopped at the gate in front of her rental house and looked up at the stars. For a moment, she pictured Jonas, sitting with his notebook, writing the first words of a story he thought had ended long ago. Then she thought of Glenn, watching from the corner, locked behind walls he didn't know how to tear down.

She didn't have the answers. But she had faith. And that was something.

❧❧❧

Grace curled up in her chair, journal in hand.

Some hearts open slowly, like flowers in the shade. But even slow-growing things bloom when they're tended to with care.

I don't know what's next for Jonas, or Glenn, or even me. But I know this: the light always finds its way in. And today, I saw it flicker to life in two unexpected places.

Maybe that's what healing is. Not fixing everything at once. Just noticing where God is moving—and moving with Him.

Chapter 8

PAGES TURNING

The leaves had started to blush at the edges, that in-between time when summer hadn't fully left but autumn was already whispering its intent as the fall equinox approached. Grace stood at the kitchen window of the rental house, watching a single crimson leaf twirl to the ground. Her journal lay open on the table behind her, half-filled pages fluttering in the breeze from the slightly cracked door.

That afternoon, Jonas had arrived at the diner earlier than usual. He looked rested, energized even. When he slid onto the stool at the counter, Grace noticed a difference—not just in his posture but in the light behind his eyes.

"You look like you've got something to say," she said, pouring his coffee.

"I might," he said, smiling. "I think I'm going to leave Harbor's End."

Grace blinked. "Oh."

"Not today. Not tomorrow. But soon. I've been praying more. Writing. Thinking. I feel like God's working something in me again. Like there's something more I need to be part of. Somewhere."

She nodded slowly. "You're not running, are you?"

"No," he said quickly. "Not this time. This feels different. Like stepping out of the boat."

She smiled. "Just don't take your eyes off Jesus."

He tapped the notebook beside his cup. "I'm trying not to. I even wrote a letter to an old friend from college who's part of a church plant in Nova Scotia. They've been looking for help."

"Wow," Grace said. "That's big."

"It is. But I want to live again, Grace. Really live."

Across the diner, Glenn sat with his usual coffee and newspaper. He wasn't reading. He was listening.

☕☕☕

The next day, Grace was folding napkins behind the counter when Glenn wandered up. He lingered longer than usual, his cup empty.

"You hear about Jonas?" he asked casually.

Grace nodded. "He feels like it's time for something new."

Glenn scratched the back of his neck. "Can't say I get it. He's got a good thing here. Quiet. Predictable."

"That's just it," Grace said gently. "Sometimes quiet and predictable isn't where growth happens."

Glenn didn't reply right away. Then, almost gruffly, he said, "Some of us prefer it that way."

"I get that," she said. "But sometimes the safe road's just the long way to loneliness."

He looked at her then, really looked. But whatever he was going to say, he swallowed it down and went back to his booth.

Later that evening, as Grace closed up, she found herself alone with Jonas again. He was finishing his pie, that familiar notebook closed beside his plate.

"Are you scared?" she asked, sliding into the booth across from him.

"Terrified," he admitted. "But I think that's how I know it's right. Faith isn't about certainty. It's about obedience."

Grace nodded. "Just promise me one thing?"

"What's that?"

"That you won't let the fear of failing stop you from trying."

He reached across the table and gently squeezed her hand. "Only if you promise the same."

Today, someone I care about decided to walk toward the unknown. Not away from something, but toward what might be. Faith looks different on everyone. For Jonas, it's a move. For Glenn, maybe just staying long enough to be seen. For me? I think it's holding space for both. Trusting that God's not finished with any of us yet.

Pages are turning. I can feel it. And this time, I'm not afraid of the next chapter.

Chapter 9

THE VISIT

The rental house smelled like apple cinnamon tea and fresh laundry when Liz stepped inside, dragging her suitcase behind her.

Grace met her at the door with a warm hug and a crooked smile. "I almost forgot how short you are."

Liz smirked. "And I forgot how bossy you are when you're cleaning."

They laughed, falling into their usual rhythm as if no time had passed at all.

Monday morning, Grace brought Liz to the diner. It was a quiet weekday morning, the kind with regulars sipping coffee and the radio humming low in the background.

"This is Maggie," Grace said, gesturing behind the counter.

Maggie wiped her hands on her apron and gave a warm nod. "Hear a lot about you. Tea?"

"All good, I hope! And I'd love a cup, thanks," Liz said.

Grace excused herself to grab a few things from the back, leaving Maggie and Liz alone at the counter for a moment.

"She's doing better, you know," Liz said softly.

Maggie nodded. "I can see it. There's light coming back to her. Doesn't ask for anything. Just shows up."

Liz took a sip of her tea. "She's always been like that. Loyal to a fault. But she's never made space for herself."

Maggie glanced toward the kitchen. "Well, she's doing it now. And she's stirring things up more than she knows."

Liz raised an eyebrow. "Glenn?"

Maggie gave a subtle smile but said nothing.

Later that day, Liz wandered into the general store while Grace was next door dropping off mail.

She found Glenn restocking canned goods in the back aisle.

"You must be Glenn," Liz said.

He turned slowly, cautious. "And you're the tea-drinker from Fredericton."

Liz smiled. "She told you that, did she?"

He gave a slight nod. "She talks about you."

"That's mutual," Liz replied. "You're not what I expected."

Glenn's posture stiffened slightly. "Meaning?"

Liz didn't flinch. "Meaning you seem like someone trying really hard not to care. And failing."

He looked away, then back. "And that's a bad thing?"

"No," Liz said softly. "It's just . . . good to see someone else who's still learning how to stay."

They stood in silence for a moment before Grace came in, waving a receipt and apologizing for taking so long.

As they left the store, Liz glanced back at Glenn and gave a slight nod. He didn't return it—not fully—but something in his shoulders eased.

***

That night, Liz and Grace sat by a window in the rental, watching the sun fall over the water.

"You've changed," Liz said.

Grace pulled the blanket tighter around her. "I feel like I'm finally becoming myself again. Or maybe for the first time."

Liz reached over and squeezed her hand. "That's what I was hoping to see."

Liz came and left like a breeze through an open window—familiar, comforting, and just long enough to stir up what needed stirring. She didn't try to fix anything. She just showed up and reminded me that I'm still becoming.

Maybe that's all we're really meant to do for each other.

Chapter 10

SOFT PLACES

The diner had that quiet lull between lunch and dinner when the sunlight turned mellow and the hum of conversation slowed to a gentle murmur. Maggie was in the back office balancing receipts. Grace wiped down the front counter before getting the mop, humming softly to herself.

Maggie emerged with a stretch and a groan. "These knees weren't made for accounting."

Grace grinned. "Mine aren't made for mopping, but here we are."

Maggie poured herself a cup of coffee and perched on a stool at the counter. "You're settling in?"

"I think so," Grace said. "Feels more familiar than it should."

Maggie studied her with a look only a seasoned woman could give—part knowing, part gentle caution. "You've got a calming way about you. People talk more when you're around."

"Sometimes they just need someone to listen."

Maggie's gaze drifted toward the corner booth, now empty. "You know, I've seen Glenn sit there nearly every afternoon for years. Same booth. Same order. Like clockwork. But these past couple of weeks?" She paused, stirring her coffee. "He's staying a little longer. Saying a little more."

Grace didn't answer right away. "He seems like someone who's had to hold a lot inside."

Maggie gave a small, almost weary smile. "He always was quiet, even as a boy. But after . . . well, after what happened with his ex, it was like he turned to stone. Not angry, just unreachable."

"I didn't realize," Grace said softly.

"I never told many people. He didn't want the whole town knowing. And most just assumed. . . ." Maggie stopped, her mouth tightening.

"That he was the problem," Grace offered gently.

She nodded. "People are quick to fill in blanks with whatever suits their narrative."

Grace looked down at the cloth in her hands. "He's not the only one who's been misunderstood."

Maggie's voice was quieter now. "Lately, I've noticed something in him. Not big, not loud. Just . . . softer edges. A little more light in his eyes." She looked over at Grace. "And I think it has something to do with the fact that you're here."

Grace blinked. "Maggie. . . ."

"I'm not matchmaking," Maggie said, holding up a hand. "I'm just grateful. He's been hiding in my diner for years. Maybe now, finally, he's starting to want more than just surviving."

***

Later that week, a late afternoon rainstorm kept most customers away. Grace was restocking napkin holders when Glenn walked in, damp from the drizzle. He didn't head for the corner. He walked right up to the counter.

"Coffee?" she asked, already reaching for the pot.

He nodded, dripping slightly. "Could use it."

She poured, then leaned on the counter. "You ever think about what you'd be doing if life had gone differently?"

He didn't answer right away. Then, "All the time. Then I stop. It doesn't help."

"Sometimes it does," she said softly. "If only to remind ourselves we're still here."

He looked at her then. Tired, guarded. But not angry. "You ever stop thinking about your husband?"

"No," she said. "But the grief softens. It doesn't go away, but it stops defining every breath."

He sipped his coffee and stared out the window. "I think I forgot who I was when I was married. Or maybe I never knew."

Grace wiped a clean glass absently. "Then maybe now's your time to find out."

***

As the rain patted softly against the roof, Grace scribbled into her journal:

> *Today was a soft day. The kind that doesn't shout or shine but hums steady in your bones. Maggie sees it. Glenn feels it. I sense it too.*
>
> *Not everything broken has to be fixed right away. Some things just need to be held gently, long enough to believe they're still worth something.*
>
> *God works in soft places too. In the quiet trust of a rainy afternoon. In a hesitant smile. In the miracle of someone walking in instead of staying away.*

Chapter 11

WHISPERS OF MORE

The scent of autumn was stronger now—crisp apples, damp leaves, and woodsmoke curling through the trees on the edge of town. Grace had begun walking to the diner each morning, bundled in a scarf and jacket, enjoying the rhythm of small-town life. It gave her time to think, to breathe.

One morning, as she passed the general store, Glenn stepped out carrying a box of canned goods. He looked surprised to see her but not displeased.

"Morning," she offered.

"Morning." He shifted the box in his arms. "You headed in early?"

She nodded. "Maggie wanted help with the delivery. Coffee truck's late again."

He hesitated. "I could drive you. Or walk with you. It's not far."

Her brows lifted slightly at the offer. "Walking's good. Clears my head."

Glenn gave a small nod and fell into step beside her, silent at first. The quiet between them wasn't awkward, though—it was comfortable, like the hush of the woods in fall.

After a while, he said, "You ever wish things had gone differently?"

"All the time," Grace replied honestly. "But I'm learning not to stay there too long."

He glanced sideways at her. "You make it look easier than it is."

She gave a short laugh. "It's not. I just talk to God a lot more than I used to."

He didn't respond at first, but she noticed his hand tighten slightly around the box.

"I used to pray," he said finally. "Before. When I thought my life made sense."

They reached the diner, and Grace unlocked the side door using the keypad. "You can still pray," she said gently. "Even if life doesn't make sense. Maybe especially then."

That afternoon, Glenn showed up again. No rain, no errand, no excuse. Just him, standing in the doorway as the late sunlight filtered through the windows.

"Need a hand?" he asked.

Grace blinked. "With what?"

He shrugged. "I don't know. Whatever you're doing."

She handed him a rag and nodded at the stack of saltshakers. "Knock yourself out."

They worked in silence for a while, wiping, refilling, straightening. Glenn paused now and then, his expression unreadable.

After a long pause, he said, "She used to say I was the kind of man no one would ever respect."

Grace looked up slowly. She didn't speak. She didn't need to.

He kept polishing a saltshaker, his voice steady. "Said I was too quiet. Too soft. Said that's why people walked all over me."

Grace didn't look away. She just nodded once, and let the moment breathe.

The silence between them settled like a quilt—heavy but not suffocating. Shared. A knowing without probing.

Eventually, he said, "Funny thing is, I started to believe her."

Grace swallowed and met his eyes. "That's how lies work. They stick to the places where we're already unsure."

He looked at her then. Not with sorrow but something rawer. Honest.

They didn't speak for a long while after that. But neither of them moved away.

He said just enough. Not everything, but enough. And it was like I could see the outline of the wound, even if he didn't name it.

Sometimes the bravest thing a person can do is let the truth rise to the surface, even if it only touches air for a second.

God doesn't need us to shout our pain. Sometimes He meets us in the hush of it, in the moment someone finally sees what we've been carrying. And stays.

Chapter 12

STEPPING OUT

The leaves had turned fully now, burnt oranges and deep reds blanketing the town in beauty and the subtle ache of change. The air carried the scent of firewood and the unmistakable feeling that things were shifting.

Grace stood behind the counter at the diner, pouring Jonas his usual afternoon coffee. He looked like a man holding both excitement and hesitation in the same breath.

"I'll be leaving soon," he said without ceremony. "Already found a place to stay."

She looked up. "Really?"

"Yeah. Couple of weeks from now. I spoke to my friend in Nova Scotia again. They're planting a church just outside of Truro. Said I could come and help however I'm needed."

Grace smiled, though it caught at the edges. "That sounds like the kind of second act you've been praying for."

He nodded. "It is. But leaving here . . . leaving you . . . it's not nothing."

"I know," she said, her voice soft. "But it's also not the end."

Jonas glanced out the window. "You know what's wild? I thought this little town was where I'd disappear. Fade out quietly. But somehow, it became the place I heard God again."

Grace swallowed, blinking back a rush of warmth in her chest. "Maybe that's what Harbor's End is meant for. A place to find your beginning."

They sat in silence for a moment. Then Jonas said, "I've written something. For you."

He pulled a folded page from his jacket pocket, worn soft by his hands. He slid it across the counter.

Grace hesitated, then opened it. It was a short letter and a poem. Simple, honest. About grief and stillness, about faith rekindled, about holding ground when everything else shifted.

"I don't know what to say," she whispered.

"Just . . . don't forget me," he said.

"Not a chance."

∎∎∎

Later that evening, Jonas stopped by the general store. Glenn was stocking shelves with his usual detached focus. When he saw Jonas, he gave a short nod.

"Grace says you're leaving."

Jonas raised an eyebrow. "Didn't know she talked about me."

"She doesn't," Glenn replied, expression unreadable. "But I notice things."

"Then yeah. I'm heading to Nova Scotia. Helping with a church plant. Crazy, right?"

Glenn grunted. "Guess it makes sense for someone like you."

Jonas smirked. "Someone like me?"

"You believe things. Follow the call."

Jonas grew quiet. "I think you believe too. You're just scared to admit it."

Glenn didn't respond. Just kept shelving.

As Jonas turned to leave, he paused. "You're braver than you think, Glenn. And she sees it. So do I."

That night, Grace stepped onto the porch of the rental house. The stars were bright, clear. She thought about how much had changed in such a short time—how she had changed.

> *Jonas is leaving. A part of me feels like I'm losing something steady, something known. But the bigger part of me? It's proud.*
>
> *Watching someone step out in faith is a holy thing. It reminds me that God is still calling people into the unknown. Still writing new stories. Even in the second half of life.*
>
> *And maybe faith isn't just about leaving or staying. Maybe it's about listening. And when the voice comes—whether it's loud or gentle—trusting that God will meet us on the road.*

Chapter 13

WHAT REMAINS

The days were shorter now. Shadows stretched longer across the sidewalks, and Grace found herself noticing how quickly the sun dipped behind the tree line in the evenings.

Jonas's decision to leave hung in the air like woodsmoke—present, lingering, and not entirely unpleasant. It was the kind of ache that comes with change you know is right but still don't want.

At the diner, Maggie had said little about it. She just worked a little quieter, her usual hum of activity softened, as if trying not to disturb something sacred. Glenn, however, had grown more restless.

He stopped by three days in a row, never staying long but always finding a reason to pass through. Sometimes it was pie. Sometimes a coffee refill. Today, it was to "fix the sticky door" at the back.

"Doesn't seem that sticky," Grace said as he tugged it open and closed a few times.

Glenn shrugged. "Better safe than sorry."

She watched him, arms crossed. "You're avoiding something."

He raised an eyebrow. "What makes you say that?"

"People usually only fix things when they're trying not to feel them."

He paused, the door halfway open. "You think you've got me figured out?"

"No," she said honestly. "But I think you've spent a lot of years keeping busy so you didn't have to face what broke."

He looked at her, a flicker of something behind his guarded stare. "And what if fixing things is the only way I know how to keep from falling apart?"

Grace didn't smile. Didn't press. Just said quietly, "Then maybe it's time someone reminded you that you don't have to do it alone."

They stood there in the echo of her words. Glenn turned back to the door, gave it one last tug, then let it close without comment.

⁂

That evening, Maggie and Grace closed up together. Maggie had grown unusually quiet.

"You okay?" Grace asked as she wiped down the counter.

Maggie hesitated, then sighed. "It's strange. Watching someone go when they've finally found peace. But it's good. It's right. I just—" she glanced toward the kitchen door "—I keep hoping maybe it'll shake something loose in Glenn too."

Grace didn't answer. She didn't need to. They both knew how tightly Glenn held on to things, especially his silence.

Maggie continued. "You know what surprised me most? How much lighter Jonas looked after he told us he was leaving. Like deciding to go gave him back his breath."

Grace nodded. "It did. Obedience does that."

Maggie gave a small laugh. "I'd forgotten that. You should come to church with me sometime. They've got a great women's group—all ages and stages. They put on a breakfast the second Saturday of each month."

Grace smiled. "That sounds like a great way for me to meet people and get myself back to church. I miss it—the community, the communal worship. I think I may take you up on that offer, Maggie. Thanks."

Later that night, Grace stepped out into the chilly air, pulling her sweater tighter around her shoulders. She looked up at the stars and thought about the people who had entered her life over the last couple of months—messy, wounded, wonderful people.

She thought about how Glenn had stood still today. Really still. Not fixing. Not fleeing. Just standing. Even if just for a moment. And somehow, that meant something.

Jonas is almost gone, but something stays behind. Maybe it's the courage to move. Maybe it's the invitation to breathe deeper.

Maggie sees it. I see it. Even Glenn feels it, though he'd never admit it. Today wasn't a grand confession. No big moment. But Glenn didn't run. He didn't cover it up with sarcasm or retreat. He stayed. And sometimes? That's a miracle too.

Maybe what remains after someone leaves isn't emptiness—but space. For someone else to rise. To heal. To believe again.

Chapter 14

THE INVITATION

It was late afternoon when Maggie dried her hands on a dish towel and leaned against the counter, watching Grace refill the sugar canisters.

"Did you go to church back home?" she asked casually, like one might ask about a favorite recipe.

Grace didn't look up right away. "I used to. After Michael died . . . it was hard. I still prayed. Read my Bible, devotionals. But I couldn't seem to sit through a service without falling apart."

Maggie nodded, her face soft. "I get that. Sometimes grief crowds out the places that used to bring peace."

Grace looked over, surprised by the gentle wisdom in the words.

"I'm not trying to push," Maggie added. "But my offer still stands . . . if you ever feel like coming with me, I'd be happy to have you. It's nothing fancy. Just an old building, creaky pews, and a handful of folks who believe God's still working in small towns."

Grace smiled faintly. "That actually sounds kind of perfect."

* * *

On Sunday morning, Grace sat beside Maggie in the third row from the back. The sanctuary smelled like old hymnals and lemon cleaner. Sunlight slanted through the stained-glass windows, catching motes of dust that danced like prayers in midair.

The service was simple. A few songs, a scripture reading, a sermon on restoration from the book of Joel—"I will restore to you the years the locusts have eaten."

The words settled deep into Grace's spirit, not like a sudden thunderclap but like water soaking into dry ground. She didn't cry. But something loosened.

Near the end of the message, she turned her head slightly—and saw him.

Jonas. Sitting alone on the far side of the sanctuary, second pew from the back. His head bowed slightly, hands folded. When the final song began, he stood slowly, quietly joined in the chorus.

And just behind him, against the back wall, half in shadow—Glenn.

He didn't sing. Didn't even remove his jacket. But he stood the entire time, still and alert.

When the service ended, Jonas caught her eye, gave her a quiet nod, and turned to leave. Glenn was already halfway out the door, slipping into the bright morning before anyone could speak.

Grace stood in the aisle for a moment longer, feeling the weight of something she couldn't name. Not resolution. Not quite hope. But motion.

God was moving.

***

That night, Grace sat at her kitchen table with the windows cracked open and the sound of the waves just audible in the distance.

I sat in a pew today, and it didn't break me. It steadied me.

There's something about joining your voice with others—even when it shakes—that makes you remember you're not alone in the story. Jonas was there. So was Glenn. Two men in motion—one stepping forward, one barely inside the door. I think God is at work in both. And maybe in me too.

Maybe healing isn't always loud. Maybe it sounds like an old hymn sung in a sunlit church by people who still believe grace is for the ones who don't feel worthy of it.

Chapter 15

BENEDICTION

The morning Jonas was set to leave, the sky blushed with the faintest pink along the horizon. Grace arrived early at the diner, unlocking the door before Maggie even got there. The place was still; coffee pot empty.

Jonas had asked for one last quiet breakfast. No fanfare. No crowd. Just coffee, eggs, and a goodbye that wasn't too hard.

He arrived with his usual smile. Grace had seen that smile change over the weeks—from worn and uncertain to full and free.

"You sure about this?" she asked as she filled two mugs.

He nodded. "I've never been more sure."

She slid into the booth across from him. "You've changed, you know."

"I know. So have you."

They ate quietly, comfortably. The kind of silence that only comes when words have already done their work.

After breakfast, Jonas stood. "I've got a long drive ahead."

Grace stood too. “Then you’d better get going.”

Jonas reached for her hand, squeezed it. “You’re a big part of why I can leave, Grace. Thank you. For reminding me of who I am.”

Tears pricked her eyes, but she held them back. “Go be who God called you to be. I’ll be right here, cheering you on.”

He walked to the door, paused, then turned back. “And Glenn?” he said.

“What about him?”

“Don’t give up on him. He’s been standing at the edge of something for a long time.”

She nodded.

Jonas gave a final wave and stepped outside. Grace followed him to the sidewalk and watched as he climbed into his old truck. He gave one last look back, a smile that said everything words couldn’t, then pulled away.

The truck rolled slowly down the main road, tires crunching sticks and gravel, taillights glowing in the early morning haze. Grace stood there until it disappeared around the bend—gone from sight but not from heart.

⁂

Later that day, Glenn appeared in the doorway just after the lunch rush. He didn’t order anything. Just stood there, hands in his jacket pockets.

“He’s really gone?” he asked.

Grace nodded.

Glenn stared out the window. “Feels quiet now.”

“It’s always quiet after someone brave leaves,” she said.

He didn’t move. “Brave,” he repeated under his breath.

Then, before she could say anything else, he turned and left.

⁂

That night, Grace sat on the porch, Jonas's poem in her lap, a blanket around her shoulders. She didn't cry; she smiled. Because when someone steps into God's call, the ache is holy.

He left before the leaves all fell. Like he didn't need to see the end of the season to know it was time. Some people come into our lives like bridges—not meant to stay, but meant to help us cross.

Jonas helped me remember that God still calls. Still speaks. Still redeems. And now, he's walking out the calling God whispered back into his heart.

As for me? I'm still here. But the ground is shifting. I can feel it. And I think Glenn can too.

Chapter 16

BETWEEN THE LINES

The days after Jonas left settled into a soft, strange quiet. Grace felt his absence like the space a book leaves when you turn the last page—you carry the story with you, but it no longer speaks aloud.

At the diner, the rhythm resumed with November's arrival. Coffee brewed. Dishes clattered. The door jingled. But something had shifted. Conversations lingered longer. Silences felt softer. And Glenn . . . Glenn kept showing up.

He was still Glenn—measured, reserved—but the edges were less sharp. He'd started sitting closer to the counter. Asking Grace how her day was. Offering to change the lightbulb in the back hallway without being asked.

He wasn't chasing connection. Just . . . not avoiding it.

One afternoon, after the lunch rush had faded into slow hours and Maggie had retreated to the office to do paperwork, Grace found herself wiping down a table near Glenn's usual seat.

He didn't move when she came around to lean on the back counter, not hovering, just present.

He looked up at her after a long sip of coffee. "You always know when to show up."

Grace gave a half-smile. "Part of the job."

A pause.

Then, without warning, Glenn said, "She hated silence."

Grace said nothing, just tilted her head, listening.

Glenn's eyes stayed on his mug. "Said it meant something was wrong. So I filled it. Even when I didn't want to. I got real good at pretending peace."

Grace stood still, quiet.

"She always made me feel like I was too much—or not enough. Like if I said the wrong thing, everything would collapse."

A moment passed.

"I stopped saying anything altogether, eventually."

The air between them was gentle. No rush. No fixing. Just presence.

Grace spoke softly. "That sounds exhausting."

He nodded once. "It was."

A quiet beat settled in.

"You've got a calm about you," he said finally. "Doesn't feel like pressure."

"I've had to learn that," Grace said. "And unlearn a few things too."

He gave a slight, tired smile. "Feels like I've got a lot of unlearning to do."

Grace folded her cleaning cloth and set it on the counter. "Sometimes it starts with one person daring to be different. And the rest follows when it's ready."

She didn't linger. Just returned to her work, letting the words sit there like an open invitation.

As she cleared tables, Grace's eyes lingered on the bulletin board near the door—cluttered with notices for bake sales, choir practice, and lost mittens. Maybe, she thought, there could be something new there. Something that brought people together for no reason other than joy.

A small craft fair, maybe—quilts, carvings, candles. Just a thought, but one that settled somewhere deep, where hope had been quiet for too long.

That evening, as the sun dipped low over the harbor, Grace found herself out on the porch, a soft breeze rustling the trees and the weight of the day settling over her shoulders like a well-worn shawl.

She opened her journal, pen tapping against the paper before the words came.

Healing comes quietly, like dusk. Not with fanfare but with shadows giving way to gentle light.

Glenn shared something today—something real. I didn't press. I didn't fix. I just stayed. Sometimes love isn't a declaration. Sometimes it's leaving space for someone else to be brave.

Chapter 17

QUIET INTENTIONS

It was a Thursday afternoon when Glenn showed up with a brown paper bag.

Grace was restocking the pie case, elbow-deep in whipped cream and cinnamon, when the door jingled and he stepped inside.

He was not in his usual jacket but in a plaid flannel rolled to the elbows. He approached the counter and held out the bag. "Figured you might not have dinner plans."

Grace raised an eyebrow. "Is this a peace offering?"

Glenn half-smiled. "It's stew. I made too much. Thought maybe you'd save me from having to eat leftovers all weekend."

Grace took the bag, still warm. "Homemade?"

"Don't sound so surprised."

She pulled the top open, inhaled. "Okay, I'm impressed."

Glenn leaned against the counter but didn't sit. "I didn't come to linger."

"I didn't ask you to," she said gently, but there was kindness in it.

He looked like he wanted to say something more, but the words didn't come. Instead, he gave a nod and turned to go.

At the door, he paused.

"I'm not great at . . . showing up," he said over his shoulder. "But I'm trying."

Grace met his eyes. "I noticed."

He nodded again, then stepped out into the cool air.

From behind the diner's front window, Grace watched him cross the street, then noticed a well-dressed woman lingering near the street corner. Younger, poised, her long coat cinched neatly at the waist. She stepped off the corner and into Glenn's path.

Grace's hand stilled on the rag she'd been cleaning up the pie case with. The exchange outside wasn't loud enough for her to hear, but the body language spoke volumes. The woman leaned in with a smile that was all too familiar, tilting her head the way people do when they've known someone for a very long time. Glenn's shoulders stiffened. He said something short, clipped, before glancing back toward the diner window. Grace instinctively stepped back, out of sight, her pulse quickening.

By the time she peeked again, the woman was brushing her hand lightly across Glenn's arm. He didn't return the gesture. Instead, he muttered something and walked away, leaving the woman standing alone, her expression unreadable.

Grace tried to shake off the image, but unease lodged itself deep. Whoever that woman was, she clearly knew Glenn. And by the look of things, not just in passing.

The bell above the diner door jingled. Grace nearly dropped the rag as the very same woman strolled in, confidence in every step. Her perfume, sharp and floral, lingered in the air. She slid onto a stool at the counter as if she belonged there.

"You must be Grace," the woman said, her smile polished and practiced. "I'm . . . an old friend of Glenn's."

Grace forced her lips into a polite curve, though her insides tightened. She nodded, setting the rag aside. "Nice to meet you."

The woman extended a perfectly manicured hand. "I'm Claire."

The name settled like a stone in Grace's stomach. She took the hand anyway, her curiosity mingling with a strange, unwelcome pang. *Old friend.* Grace wondered if those two words carried more history than she was prepared to hear.

Later that evening, Grace heated the stew on the stovetop. It was rich, layered, full of flavor in slow time. *Like him,* she thought. *Simple on the surface, but deeper than he let on.*

She ate in silence, the kind that felt like a blessing.

Today he brought stew. Not flowers. Not flattery. Just something warm and homemade, left without expectation. There are gestures that don't shout but still say, "I see you." Maybe that's the most sacred kind.

And yet, after he left, I caught sight of someone else. A woman waiting for him on the street—younger, polished, with the kind of confidence that makes me feel suddenly older than I am. Later she walked into the diner and introduced herself as "an old friend." The words linger, though I don't know what they mean. Still, I felt the pang. A reminder that his story didn't begin with me, and maybe it won't end with me either.

I don't know where this road leads. I'm not trying to name it too soon. But I know what courage looks like when it walks through a diner door with shaking hands and something offered. And I'm learning to receive without running—even when shadows from the past brush close.

Chapter 18

OPEN DOORS

The morning light filtered through the diner windows, soft and silver. Maggie was humming to herself near the griddle, flipping pancakes, the rhythm of the spatula steady and sure.

Grace topped off the creamers and tried not to think about the silence that had followed Claire's sudden reappearance the day before. Glenn hadn't been in yet today.

The sound of the bell over the door jingled once, twice, before she realized it was her phone ringing, not the door.

Grace didn't immediately recognize the number on the screen, but she answered.

"Hello?" she said, wiping her hands on her apron.

"Grace Templeton?" The voice on the other end was familiar, warm with a lilt of surprise. "It's Carol from Maple Grove District. I hope I'm not catching you at a bad time."

Grace blinked. "Oh, Carol! No, not at all. It's been ages."

Carol laughed softly. "It has. Listen, I'll get right to the point. We've had a sudden opening for the coordinator position, the one we had talked about this past summer. Your name came up right away. I heard you're out East now, but if you'd consider coming back, we'd love to have you."

For a moment, the diner faded—the clink of dishes, the low murmur of customers, Maggie's humming—all of it blurred beneath the weight of that word: *back*.

Back.

Back to familiarity.

Back to the version of herself she thought she'd outgrown.

"I . . . I don't know what to say," Grace managed.

"Just think about it," Carol said gently. "I'll email the details. We'd need to know before winter break starts so we could get you set up for the new year."

They exchanged goodbyes, and when Grace hung up, her hand lingered on the phone.

Maggie turned from the griddle. "Everything all right, dear?"

Grace forced a smile. "Yes. Just . . . unexpected news." She paused for a moment. "You know," Grace said, turning back toward Maggie, "there's so much talent in this town. The woodworking, the knitting, the baking . . . it seems a shame we don't showcase it."

Maggie's brows lifted. "You thinking of organizing something?"

"Maybe. A little craft show—something simple. Just a way for folks to gather."

Maggie smiled. "That sounds like you, Grace. Always finding ways to make people feel they belong."

Later, when the diner emptied and the coffee had gone cold, Grace stood by the window, looking out toward the distant line of trees that marked the start of the marina trail.

She wondered if Glenn had walked it today.

She wondered if he'd walked it alone.

Today I was offered a way back. Back to the familiar, the steady, the safe.

I should feel grateful—maybe even relieved. Instead, I feel torn. Like someone offered me an old coat that used to fit but now hangs differently across my shoulders.

Part of me misses that version of life—the predictability, the respect, the certainty of purpose. But another part whispers that maybe God brought me here for reasons that haven't fully unfolded yet.

I don't know what I'll say. But I do know this—peace doesn't always look like comfort. Sometimes it looks like staying still long enough to see what God is doing right where you are.

Chapter 19

TESTIMONY

The fellowship hall smelled of cinnamon buns and brewed coffee that Saturday morning. Folding chairs scraped softly against the linoleum as women shuffled to their seats, murmuring greetings and laughter.

Grace sat near the end of a long table, palms pressed together in her lap, waiting. She hadn't been in a room like this since Michael died. The sound of worship music playing quietly from a small speaker felt both comforting and foreign all at once, like stepping into an old, familiar song but not knowing if you could still sing along.

When the pastor's wife welcomed everyone and mentioned that there would be a time later for sharing a brief testimony or two about God's faithfulness, Grace felt her chest tighten. She stared at the paper doily beneath her coffee mug, willing her breath to slow.

Maggie leaned over and squeezed Grace's hand. "You don't have to," she whispered. Then softer still, "But you do have a story worth sharing."

Grace swallowed. She had told parts of her story before—snippets to strangers, fragments to friends—but never like this, never in a room full of people she barely knew. Still, something in Maggie's eyes steadied her.

During the break before the program began, Grace rose and crossed the room to the pastor's wife. Her voice wavered at first, then settled. "If you're still looking for someone to share," she said quietly, "I'd be willing."

The pastor's wife soon approached the podium, and Maggie, bustling between tables with a coffeepot, caught Grace's eye and gave her an encouraging nod. "You'll be fine," she mouthed.

Then, "Good morning everyone. I'd like to introduce you to Grace Templeton, new to Harbor's End."

A polite ripple of applause moved through the room. Grace rose slowly and approached the front of the room, smoothing her sweater. Her heart fluttered but her voice, when it came, surprised her by being steady.

"Good morning," she began. "I'm not used to speaking like this, but when Maggie invited me to come today, I felt like I was supposed to say yes." She paused, glancing at the women's expectant faces. "A little over a year ago, I lost my husband, Michael. We had built a life together in Ontario, and when he passed, everything I thought I was, every plan I had, just . . . stopped."

The room went quiet. Grace breathed, clasping her hands tighter.

"I didn't lose my faith, but I did lose my footing. For months, I wondered if God had forgotten me, or if I had somehow stepped out of His plan. Coming here, to Harbor's End, was my way of listening again. Of seeing if He still had more for me than grief."

A few women nodded. One reached for a tissue.

"I don't have all the answers," Grace continued, "but I know this: God meets us in our wilderness. Sometimes it looks like a quiet town by the ocean. Sometimes it looks like a diner full of strangers who start to feel like family. And sometimes, it looks like showing up at a breakfast like this, trembling but willing."

Her voice softened. "If you're in a hard season right now, I want you to know, He hasn't forgotten you. He's not done writing your story. I'm learning that myself, one small step at a time."

When she sat down, Maggie refilled her coffee with a proud smile. Around the room, murmured *amens* and gentle applause filled the air. Grace felt a warmth rise in her chest—not applause for her but the sense that God was still weaving something, even here.

Glenn hadn't planned on being here. He'd driven Maggie to the church that morning so she wouldn't have to worry about parking on icy streets, and then he wandered inside when he saw the hall buzzing with activity. He told himself he'd just stand at the back and wait until it was over. Nobody would notice a man leaning against the doorway anyway.

But he noticed Grace.

From his spot near the coat rack, Glenn watched her stand to speak. Her voice was gentle but clear, like the tide against the rocks. The words about losing her husband, about God not being finished with her yet, they landed somewhere deep inside him. He realized, uncomfortably, that he was holding his breath.

She wasn't trying to impress anyone. She wasn't even looking around for approval. She was simply telling the truth.

Glenn felt a flicker of something he hadn't let himself feel in years—admiration that wasn't tinged with fear or obligation or control. He saw her hands tremble as she spoke but also saw the steadiness in her eyes. And for the first time, he wondered what it would mean to stand beside a woman like that. Not to own her, not to fix her, but to walk with her.

With his ex's arrival back in town, he'd been torn in ways he hated to admit. Part of him still carried the old questions: *Had she really changed? Was forgiveness the same thing as starting over? Could history be rewritten if she were smiling and contrite enough?* But the memories were never far—words sharpened to wounds, silences that cut deeper than shouting, nights he'd prayed for escape. He couldn't pretend those scars weren't there.

And then there was Grace. Different. Quieter. Stronger in ways she didn't seem to recognize herself. He caught himself wondering if he was a fool to even think she'd notice him. What if she only saw a man too shy, too broken, too cautious? Still, the thought lingered, persistent and dangerous: *What if she did?*

As the women applauded softly and Grace sat down, he caught Maggie's eye as she glanced up and across the room toward him. She smiled a knowing smile, the kind only a mother can give. Glenn shifted, heat rising in his neck, and looked away. He wasn't ready for questions, not yet. But he didn't leave either.

He stayed there, listening as the closing prayer rose like a hush over the room, thinking about her words: *He hasn't forgotten you. He's not done writing your story.*

Chapter 20

THE LONGEST PRAYER

The last customer left just after 6 o'clock. A quiet Tuesday, rain tapping steadily on the windows and fog settling in low around the harbor. Grace flipped the sign to *Closed* and turned the lock, the diner bathed in the soft hum of fluorescent light and the clatter of dishes from the back.

Maggie emerged from the kitchen, drying her hands, apron spotted with oil and flour.

"Slow day," she said, setting the towel aside.

Grace nodded. "Some days are like that."

They sat together at the counter, steaming mugs in hand—Grace with coffee, Maggie with a familiar blend of chamomile and lemon.

For a while, they didn't speak. Just sat in the kind of silence that felt earned.

Then Maggie said, "He was always a quiet boy, you know."

Grace glanced over.

"Glenn," Maggie clarified. "Soft-hearted. Quiet. Thoughtful. Took everything in—sometimes too much. His dad was the opposite. Loud, hard edges. I used to worry Glenn would disappear in the noise."

Grace listened, saying nothing.

"I hear we had a visitor yesterday," Maggie said, cautiously reading Grace's expression. "Introduced herself as 'an old friend' of Glenn's?"

Grace's eyes darted to meet Maggie's, silently confirming who the young woman was.

"When he met her," Maggie continued, "he thought he'd found someone who understood him. She was sweet as sugar when they dated. Everyone loved her. Especially the church folks." Maggie paused. "I saw pieces of him fade after they married. Slowly. Like watching color leach out of fabric."

Grace's eyes softened. "That must have been hard."

"It was worse not being able to say anything. You try warning your grown son about his wife?" She chuckled dryly. "He thought I was just being a mother hen."

"Was she . . . cruel?"

Maggie stared down into her tea. "Not in ways the world would recognize. Not at first. She broke him with words, with silence, with twisting things until he didn't trust his own thoughts. By the time she left, he didn't think he was worth loving anymore."

Grace exhaled slowly.

"I prayed for him every night after she left," Maggie said, voice quieter now. "Not for someone to come along and rescue him. Just for God to remind him that he was still worth knowing."

She looked at Grace then, eyes wise and unafraid.

"And I don't think it's a coincidence that you showed up when you did."

Grace shook her head, barely above a whisper. "I didn't come looking for any of this."

"Doesn't mean God didn't send you."

They sat for a moment, the weight of the truth between them.

Maggie smiled. "I know better than to push. Glenn's got to make his own way. But, Grace. . . ." She leaned in a little. "You're good for him. Just by being here."

Grace blinked away the sting in her eyes. "I don't want to be someone's second chance just because I'm . . . kind."

"You're not a second chance," Maggie said. "You're an answer to a long, long prayer."

Grace hesitated, "You remember that call I got the other day from back home?"

Maggie nodded.

"It was from a woman I had met at a conference this past summer. She's offered me a job, a job that I thought was my dream job. But the thought of leaving here, now. . . ." Her voice trailed off.

Maggie didn't rush to fill the silence. She simply poured another cup of tea and waited.

Finally, she said, "You know, Grace, sometimes God opens a door not to send us through it but to see if we'll pause long enough to ask Him first."

Grace looked down, tracing the rim of her mug. "So you think I shouldn't go?"

"I think," Maggie said softly, "that the place you're meant to be will still be there when your heart's ready. But if you run ahead of God, you might miss what He's still finishing right here."

Grace nodded slowly, eyes glistening. "I just don't want to make the wrong choice."

Maggie reached across the counter, her hand warm and steady over Grace's. "The right choice isn't always the easiest one, dear. But peace has a sound—quiet, sure, and gentle. You'll know it when it comes."

❦❦❦

That night, Grace walked home through the misty air, Maggie's words trailing behind her like fog.

Today I learned that love doesn't always start with sparks. Sometimes it begins with small, steady faithfulness. Showing up. Listening. Stirring soup and refilling mugs. Praying when no one's watching.

Now there's this job offer—the kind of opportunity I used to dream about. The kind that once would've made me feel seen, important, needed. But the thought of leaving here . . . of leaving them . . . it tugs at something deeper than ambition.

Maggie said peace has a sound—quiet, sure, and gentle. I keep listening for it, but tonight all I hear is my own uncertainty.

Maybe this isn't about choosing a job or a town. Maybe it's about learning to stay still long enough to let God finish what He started in me.

And maybe, just maybe, I'm right where I'm meant to be.

Chapter 21

ONE STEP FORWARD

It had been two weeks since Jonas left Harbor's End.

The diner still carried echoes of him—his corner stool, his unfinished crossword folded neatly and sitting in the magazine rack, his name scrawled on the bottom of the regulars' coffee tally sheet. Grace found herself reaching for an extra mug some mornings before catching herself.

But the ache was gentler now. Like the soft throb of a bruise nearly healed.

Glenn came in almost daily now—always in the afternoon, always sitting at the counter now. He never stayed long, and he still brought his guarded silences with him, but the sharp edges continued to dull. He watched, listened. And sometimes, when Grace laughed with Maggie or hummed while wiping down the menus, she caught the flicker of a smile trying to find its way to his face. He never mentioned Claire, and no one else brought her up either.

❧❧❧

It was Tuesday when it happened.

The rain had finally stopped, leaving behind a sky that looked like worn denim and air that smelled like wet leaves and pine.

Glenn lingered at the counter after Maggie had stepped out for her usual midafternoon walk.

Grace poured his refill, then leaned on the counter across from him. “You’re braver than most, coming out in this weather.”

He glanced toward the window. “I don’t mind the quiet days.”

“I don’t either,” she said. “You notice things you’d miss otherwise.”

Glenn tapped the side of his mug. “You ever walk the trail behind the old marina?”

“Not yet,” she said. “I’ve seen the sign, though. Maggie said it’s a nice view at the top.”

He nodded. “There’s a bench up there. Faces the water.”

They sat in the quiet that followed. He didn’t look at her, just kept his gaze on the swirling coffee in his cup.

“Sometimes I go up there to think,” he said after a moment. “Clear my head.”

Grace waited.

Glenn took a slow breath. “I thought maybe . . . you’d want to walk it with me sometime.”

She didn’t answer right away. Not because she was surprised but because she knew what it cost him to ask.

Finally, she smiled. “Sure. I’d like that.”

He looked up then, and something unspoken passed between them. Not a declaration, not a turning point. Just a *step*. A willingness to meet each other where they were.

❧❧❧

Later, as Grace wiped down the counter after Glenn had gone, a question slipped in like a draft under the door. Had he ever taken Claire up there? Had she sat on that same bench, heard him speak in that same quiet tone? And now that she was back, were they talking again, picking up pieces Grace had no claim to?

She pressed the rag harder against the counter, willing the thoughts away. It wasn't fair to wonder, and yet the wondering came all the same.

That evening, at home, Grace lit a candle and sat at her little writing desk by the window. The sky outside was streaked with deep blue and gold.

Today Glenn asked me to go for a walk. Not a grand gesture. Just an invitation into his quiet.

I think that's how trust grows. Not through speeches or sudden revelations but through showing up in small ways, again and again.

And yet, I can't help but wonder. Has he asked someone else before me to sit on that bench overlooking the water? Now that she's back, does she still linger in his thoughts the way she lingers in mine?

Still, sometimes love doesn't start with fireworks. Sometimes it starts with footsteps on a pine-needled trail and two people learning how to be brave enough to hope again.

Chapter 22

THE TRAIL

Later that week, Grace was wiping down the counter after the lunch rush when Maggie came out from the kitchen, drying her hands on a towel. The diner was quiet except for the clink of silverware from a single booth.

Maggie leaned against the counter, studying Grace with that same half-smile she'd given Glenn across the room at the women's breakfast.

"You know," she said casually, "you had quite an audience at the women's breakfast."

Grace looked up. "Oh?"

Maggie nodded. "Someone else slipped in. Didn't stay for the muffins, though."

Grace tilted her head. "Who?"

"Glenn." Maggie said it like it was no big deal, but her eyes twinkled. "He brought me, then stood in the back. Didn't think you saw him."

Grace blinked. A tiny flutter started in her chest. "I . . . didn't. He didn't say anything."

"No," Maggie said softly. "But he listened. Really listened."

Grace busied herself with stacking coffee cups to hide the warmth creeping up her neck. She wasn't sure what to do with that knowledge—the image of him leaning against the doorway, hearing her story. Part of her was grateful; part of her felt exposed.

Maggie reached over and squeezed her hand. "Sometimes people need to hear a testimony before they can offer their own," she murmured, then went back to the kitchen, leaving Grace alone with the quiet clatter of her thoughts.

The trailhead behind the marina was marked by a crooked wooden sign and a scattering of pine needles across the path. Grace pulled her scarf tighter as the late afternoon wind rustled through the trees, the possibility of snow ever present now. Glenn stood just ahead, hands in his jacket pockets, waiting.

"Didn't think you'd show," he said as she approached.

"Didn't think you'd ask," she replied, smiling.

They started walking. The ground was soft beneath their feet, and the air smelled like damp earth and spruce. For a while, they didn't speak—the silence between them filled with birdsong and the steady crunch of gravel.

When they reached the clearing near the top, Glenn gestured toward the bench.

"This is it."

Grace sat slowly, taking in the view—open sky, the grey shimmer of the bay below, and the wind brushing the tall grass like fingers through hair.

"It's beautiful," she said.

He nodded, standing beside her.

"I used to come here when things got too loud in my head. Before. During. After."

Grace didn't press. She let the wind fill the space.

"I'd sit here and ask God what was wrong with me," he said eventually. "Why someone who said she loved me made me feel so small."

Grace turned her face toward him but still said nothing.

"I stopped asking eventually. Figured maybe I just didn't deserve anything better."

"That's not true," she said quietly.

Glenn gave a small shrug. "Some days I almost believe that now."

A long pause.

"Being around you," he said, "it's like remembering something I forgot. Like . . . maybe I'm not broken beyond repair."

Grace felt a lump rise in her throat, but she kept her voice steady. "You're not."

They didn't hold hands. Didn't hug. Just sat side by side as the sun dipped lower, lighting the clouds in soft gold.

When they stood to leave, Glenn walked beside her all the way down the trail. They reached the bottom, pine needles clinging to their shoes. Grace felt lighter than she had in a long time, the sound of the waves still in her ears, the warmth of Glenn's quiet presence steady beside her.

But then she saw her.

Claire stood by the trailhead, arms folded loosely, a smile playing at her lips. The late sun caught her hair, making her look polished, prepared—like she'd been waiting.

"Glenn," Claire's voice rang sweet, familiar, threaded with a confidence that sent a chill through Grace. "There you are. I thought maybe you'd gone out of town."

Glenn froze mid-step. "Claire . . . what are you doing here?"

"I knew this was your spot," she said, glancing toward the trail behind them. "Figured if I waited long enough, I'd find you." Her gaze flicked to Grace then, lingering just a heartbeat too long. "I don't think we've met. I'm Claire—an old friend of Glenn's."

Claire obviously didn't remember meeting her at the diner, with the same introduction. Grace managed a polite nod, but her stomach tightened. *Old friend.* The words carried weight, unspoken history pressed into every syllable.

Claire turned back to Glenn, softening her tone, almost pleading but with a thread of possession. "My car won't start. Could you give me a ride home? We need to talk. Just the two of us."

The air seemed to shift, the peace of the walk dissolving. Grace stepped back slightly, unsure if she should excuse herself, unsure if she even wanted to hear his answer.

Glenn's jaw tightened. His eyes darted from Claire to Grace, as if the ground itself had tilted beneath him. For the first time in years, he was caught between the woman who had once broken him and the one who made him wonder if God was offering him something new.

Today I learned that Glenn heard my story at the women's breakfast. I didn't even know he was there. To be seen when I wasn't aware of it—especially in my faith—leaves me strangely unsettled. What did he hear? What did he think? Part of me longs to know, and part of me fears the answer.

This new knowledge, like the trail, curved like a question I didn't know I needed to ask. And the answer? It wasn't spoken—it was shown.

On a bench. In silence. In a man choosing to share something fragile instead of hiding behind his walls.

But tonight, that same man drove another woman home. Claire. Young, beautiful, sure of herself in ways I never was. Watching them leave together left me caught between hope and doubt, as if the ground I'd just found beneath my feet might give way at any moment.

Today was a step, but I can't tell if it was forward or backward. Maybe both. Maybe love is supposed to feel this risky. Or maybe I've been fooling myself all along. All I know is that my heart is restless, and the question I keep asking is whether God is leading me here—or back to the life I left behind.

Chapter 23

THE LOOK IN HIS EYES

The diner was slow the next day, the kind of quiet afternoon where the coffee pot was more background music than necessity. Grace was wiping down the booths when the bell above the door jingled.

Glenn stepped inside, jacket damp from the ocean air, hair tousled from the wind. His eyes scanned the room and landed on her.

She smiled tentatively. "Coffee?"

He nodded and sat at the counter, his usual seat. When she slid the mug in front of him, he surprised her by speaking first.

"Thanks . . . for yesterday."

Grace leaned lightly on the counter. "It was a good walk."

He nodded slowly. "I haven't brought anyone up there before. Not since . . . well, not ever."

She softened. "That place means something to you."

"It does." He traced a finger along the rim of the mug. "And it didn't feel heavy being there this time."

"That's good."

There was something new in his eyes—something less guarded, more grounded. Like the smallest hinge had shifted open.

He took a sip, then looked at her. "You make it easier. Talking, I mean."

Grace met his gaze. "You don't have to say much. Just show up."

He smiled. Not wide, but real.

But as Grace turned to refill the sugar jar, her mind caught on the memory of Claire at the bottom of the trail, waiting, smiling like she belonged there. Glenn hadn't mentioned her, and Grace didn't ask. Still, the thought lingered like a ripple on the water, disturbing what had once been calm—reminding her that hope was fragile and not hers alone to hold.

We walked the trail yesterday. And today, he came back.

I think that's the part I'll remember most—not the view or the conversation, but the way he kept showing up. And not just to the bench or the diner—but to his own life.

There's a strength in softening. A kind of courage that looks like quiet trust. And maybe, just maybe, that's the kind of love that lasts. Slowly built on a solid foundation, not rooted in old wounds and mere familiarity. Would I be crazy to pass this up?

Chapter 24

A LIGHT LEFT ON

The leaves had deepened to rust and gold, curling at the edges like the pages of an old book. Grace swept the diner steps, the bristles brushing away the damp reminder that another storm had passed through overnight.

Inside, the warmth of coffee and chatter slowly filled the room. Maggie was visiting her friend at the retirement home that week, so Grace had been opening on her own.

At precisely 9:07 a.m., Glenn walked in. Not at the end of the day. Not for five quiet minutes. *In the morning.*

Grace raised an eyebrow. “This is new.”

He shrugged, a sheepish smile tugging at his mouth. “Figured you’d be swamped without your backup.”

She handed him a mug. “Well, look at you. Coming to the rescue.”

He smirked and sat on the stool. “I’ll try not to make it a habit.”

But she knew—and maybe he knew—that he already had.

That afternoon, they worked quietly in tandem. Glenn fixed a loose hinge on the swinging kitchen door while Grace restocked napkins and refilled ketchup bottles. When their paths crossed, there were no awkward silences, just gentle conversation and occasional shared laughter.

Later, after the lunch rush, he lingered again. Grace found him in the booth by the window, staring out at the harbor.

She slid in across from him.

"Thinking about leaving town?" she teased.

He looked surprised. "What makes you say that?"

"That stare. Jonas used to get it. Like he was already seeing something beyond the water."

Glenn shook his head. "No. I'm not looking past it. Just . . . looking *into* it. Trying to see what's still here."

Grace leaned back, letting his words settle. Did he know about the job offer? Had Maggie mentioned it to him? Was he contemplating getting back together with Claire?

"I used to think my life ended when. . . ." He paused, searching for the right way to say it. "When the marriage fell apart. But now I wonder if that was just the wrong path with the wrong person. Broken."

Grace smiled softly. "God's funny like that. He does a lot with broken things."

He looked at her then. "Doesn't make it easy."

"No," she agreed. "But it's worth it."

He held her gaze for a beat too long, then glanced away. "You ever think about what's next?"

Grace tilted her head. "Next, like. . . ?" Still wondering if he knew about the possibility of her returning to Ontario.

"I don't know," he said. "The rest of it. The part where you don't just pass through town. The part where you stay."

She studied him for a moment. Then said, "Sometimes I do."

He nodded, lips pressing into a line. "Me too."

***

That night, as Grace closed the blinds in the little rental house, she caught sight of the porch light on at Maggie's next door. Though Maggie was gone for a few more days, the timer must've still been set.

The glow felt like comfort. Like invitation.

He came in this morning. Stayed longer than he had to. And for the first time, I didn't feel like we were circling something—we were slowly stepping toward it.

Not romance. Not yet. But maybe restoration. Two people learning to live again, one small act of presence at a time. But, Claire. I'm longing to know what is happening there. Why was she back? Why now? Was Glenn going to be charmed and swayed back? Where would this leave me?

Some days feel like shadows. But tonight, it feels like someone left a light on.

Chapter 25

NOTICING THINGS

Grace was refilling saltshakers when she noticed the flowers. They were sitting in a mason jar at the counter—simple, unassuming wildflowers. Nothing fancy. But fresh. Picked that morning, judging by the way the petals held dew at their edges.

She looked around. Glenn was in his usual booth, reading the local paper like it actually mattered.

She walked over, the jar in her hands.

"These yours?"

He didn't look up. "Maybe."

She waited.

"Figured the place could use something that wasn't ketchup red or pickle green."

Grace smiled, tucking the jar beside the pie display. "Well, thank you. They're lovely."

"I almost walked right past them," he said quietly. "Then I thought, *Grace would notice these.*"

That made her pause.

He was noticing what she noticed.

And maybe that meant he was noticing *her*.

⁂

That afternoon, they took their time closing up the diner. Glenn stayed behind, helping Grace stack chairs and mop the floor. It had become part of their rhythm—unscheduled but expected.

"I was thinking," he said, pausing mid-sweep, "about what you said the other day."

She looked up from the cash drawer. "You'll have to narrow it down. I say a lot of things."

"You said God does a lot with broken things."

She nodded. "Still believe it."

"So do I," he said. "Most days."

Grace leaned against the counter, watching him.

"Sometimes it's hard to imagine anything good coming out of pain. Especially when the pain keeps echoing."

He didn't speak for a moment. Then, "My ex once told me I was the kind of man no one would ever fight for."

Grace's heart stilled.

Glenn set the mop aside and leaned on it like a cane. "I carried that with me a long time. Still do, especially these days. But lately . . . I wonder if maybe she just didn't know what fighting for someone really meant."

Grace didn't move closer. Didn't reach out. But she met his eyes with gentle strength.

"She was wrong."

He didn't respond right away. Just looked at her like someone still deciding whether to believe it.

Grace continued wiping down the counter, and Glenn hesitated before sitting at a stool closer to Grace.

"She's been calling, wanting to talk," he said finally, voice low.

Grace didn't need to ask who. "Claire?"

He nodded. "She says she's just visiting her aunt in town for a bit. But Claire never just does anything."

Grace set the cloth down. "That must stir up a lot."

"Yeah," he said, staring into his coffee. "Mostly memories I'd rather leave buried." He took a breath. "But I'm not the same man I was when she left. I don't owe her my peace anymore."

Something in Grace eased. "Then hold onto it. It's worth keeping."

He looked at her, a flicker of gratitude softening his features. "That's the plan."

Grace smiled faintly. "Plans have a way of being tested." She still couldn't bring herself to tell him about the job offer.

"Guess we'll see how this one holds," he said. But his tone wasn't defensive; it was resolute.

Grace sat on the edge of her bed, journal open in her lap.

Today someone brought me flowers. Simple ones. But chosen.

There's something sacred about being seen. Not praised. Not chased. Just . . . noticed. He thinks he's not worth fighting for. But I think healing comes, not all at once, but like spring—through small, steady signs that life is still possible.

And love, maybe, too.

God, what am I supposed to do?

Chapter 26

SOMETHING IN THE AIR

Maggie returned to Harbor's End after her visit with a friend at the retirement home—with a tin of her friend's homemade molasses cookies and a raised eyebrow.

Grace was wiping down the counters when she walked in, her suitcase still rolling behind her.

"You don't even give a girl time to miss you," Grace teased.

Maggie smirked. "This place falls apart without me. Or so I tell myself."

She looked around, taking in the spotless floors, the neatly stocked pie case, and the fresh flowers at the counter.

"You've been busy," she said.

Grace shrugged. "It helps pass the time."

Maggie opened the back fridge, paused, and glanced toward the prep shelf. "And someone fixed the kitchen door hinge."

Grace didn't answer right away.

Maggie smiled slightly. "Did Glenn stop by a few times while I was gone?"

Grace gave a soft laugh. "He might've."

Maggie sat down on a stool, not pushing. "He left his thermos here once years ago and wouldn't step foot in the place for two weeks out of sheer stubbornness. But now I'm seeing little signs he's softening. That's not nothing."

Grace gave a small smile. "We've talked. He's letting some walls down."

Maggie nodded. "It shows."

She looked at Grace, expression turning more thoughtful. "I was worried he'd stay stuck forever. But you've brought something into his life. Not flashy. Just . . . steady. God knows he needed that."

"I'm not trying to fix him," Grace said gently.

"I know," Maggie replied. "That's probably why it's working."

Maggie asked, "Have you mentioned the job offer to Glenn yet?"

Grace looked up at Maggie as though she were a child just scolded. "No, not yet."

"You really ought to," Maggie said gently but firmly. "He deserves to know, especially if you decide to head back."

Grace sighed, twisting the dish towel in her hands. "I don't even know what I've decided. I keep thinking about what it would mean to go back—the security, the familiar faces, the comfort of being *useful* again."

Maggie wiped her hands on a towel, the corners of her eyes softening. "You've both been through enough silence for one lifetime, Grace. Don't add more to it."

Grace sighed, her voice low. "I don't even know what to say. I don't want him to think I'm running away . . . or that he's the reason I'd stay."

Maggie gave a small, knowing smile. "Then tell him exactly that. You don't owe him a promise—just the truth. God does His best work in the light, not in what we keep hidden."

Grace nodded slowly, eyes glistening. "I guess I'm just scared. Every time I start to trust something good, it feels like it slips through my fingers."

Maggie reached across the counter and gave her hand a squeeze. "That's not loss, honey, that's God reminding you to hold things open-handed. If it's meant to stay, it will. And if not, you'll still be okay. You've got roots here now, whether you realize it or not."

Grace swallowed hard, a small smile tugging at her lips. "You always know what to say."

Maggie chuckled softly. "Not always. But I've lived long enough to know when God's stirring something in the air—and I'd say He's not finished with you yet."

***

That evening, Grace found Glenn waiting outside the diner as she locked up.

"Hey," he said.

"Hey."

He glanced toward the marina. "You free for a walk?"

Grace smiled. "Sure."

They walked in companionable silence, the scent of salt and pine between them.

At the curve near the old lighthouse, Glenn spoke.

"My mom's back."

"Yes," Grace said. "She brought cookies."

He chuckled. "That sounds about right."

They stood still for a while, watching the last of the light settle on the water.

Then Glenn said, "She told me once she thought I'd never be happy again."

Grace didn't answer, just let him continue.

"But tonight, I think maybe I am. Or . . . I could be."

He looked at her.

And though he didn't take her hand, or say the words out loud, something passed between them again—something real and reverent.

Grace swallowed, but the lump in her throat wouldn't clear. Her heart was pounding as she struggled to find the words to start the conversation she knew was long overdue. But the words just wouldn't come.

Maggie sees more than she lets on. And maybe that's the kind of love we all need—not the kind that pushes or presumes, but the kind that gently shines a light and lets us walk into it when we're ready.

How am I going to decide whether to stay or return home? How am I going to bring this up with Glenn? I know I need to tell him, but I just can't bring myself to do it just yet.

Chapter 27

MISSED TIMING

The dinner rush had slowed to a hum. A few locals lingered over pie and coffee, their laughter low and familiar. Maggie had gone to the back to start the closing prep, leaving Grace at the counter, drying mugs that didn't really need drying.

When the bell over the door jingled, she didn't have to look up to know it was him.

Glenn's presence always carried a kind of stillness—not heavy, but grounding, like the pause before rain.

He hesitated near the door before taking his usual seat.

Grace forced her hands to steady. "Evening," she said softly.

"Evening." His voice was tired but kind.

She poured his coffee, the steam curling between them like something alive. "Long day?" she asked.

He nodded. "Long week." He didn't elaborate, and she didn't ask.

The silence stretched, not uncomfortable, but weighted—like they were both waiting for someone to name what had changed.

Finally, Glenn cleared his throat. "I heard you got a call from back home."

Grace blinked. "Maggie told you?"

He nodded, eyes on his cup. "She mentioned it. Said they offered you a good position."

"She shouldn't have," Grace murmured, then sighed. "But yes. They did."

He nodded again, slow. "That's . . . something, Grace. You've worked hard for that."

Something about the way he said her name—careful, restrained—caught her off guard. She searched his face for a flicker of what he wasn't saying, but all she saw was weariness.

"Are you happy for me?" she asked before she could stop herself.

Glenn's eyes lifted to hers. "Of course I am." But his tone was quiet, the words landing somewhere between truth and ache.

She tried to smile, but it faltered. "It's strange," she said. "The thing I prayed for before I left Ontario . . . it's here now. But I'm not sure I'm the same person who asked for it."

He nodded once, like he understood too well. "Sometimes God waits until we stop clinging to something before He gives it back."

Grace studied him. "Is that what happened with Claire?"

The question slipped out—not cruelly but gently, like a truth long waiting in the wings.

Glenn's jaw tightened. He stared into his coffee. "She says she's changed."

"And do you believe her?"

He was quiet for a long time. "I want to," he said finally. "But wanting and trusting aren't the same thing."

Grace nodded, her throat tight.

He looked up then—not at her but past her, toward the window where the reflection of the diner lights flickered across the glass. "You and I . . . ." He hesitated. "We found something steady in the middle of all this. I don't want to lose that."

Grace swallowed hard. "Neither do I."

But when he stood to leave, neither of them reached for the other.

He touched the brim of his cap, the gesture small, almost reverent. "Take care of yourself, Grace."

And then he was gone—the bell above the door jingling like punctuation on a sentence she didn't want to end.

Tonight, the air felt like the pause before a storm.

Glenn came by. We talked—or maybe we didn't. Maybe we just stood on opposite sides of a conversation neither of us was ready to finish.

I think I saw the flicker of something real in his eyes—fear, maybe, or faith, the kind that doesn't quite know which way to turn.

He said he didn't want to lose what we've found, but I don't know what we've found anymore.

Maybe that's what faith really is—holding still in the in-between, when your heart wants to run but your soul whispers:

Wait.

Chapter 28

THE DRIVE

The rain had just started again, a soft patter against the windshield that blurred the lights of Harbor's End into watercolor smudges. Glenn's hands rested on the steering wheel long after he'd parked outside his mother's house. He hadn't planned on driving anywhere tonight, but sometimes sitting still made the noise in his head too loud to ignore.

Claire's return had stirred up ghosts he thought he'd buried. But now, after days of silence and restless thoughts, one truth kept pressing at his chest—he was tired of living afraid.

He thought about Grace. Her quiet steadiness. Her laughter. The way she listened like every word mattered. She never tried to fix him, never demanded he be more than he was. But somehow, around her, he wanted to be.

He turned the keys again and started driving. Not toward Claire's Aunt's house but toward the diner. The lights were off—Grace had already gone home. Still, he pulled up, the familiar sign swaying in the wind.

"God," he murmured, his voice breaking in the empty car. "I don't want to miss what You're doing because I'm scared. Help me do this right—not out of loneliness or guilt, but because You're leading."

⁂

The next morning, Maggie noticed something different when Glenn came in. He looked the same, but there was a steadiness in his step, a quiet certainty in his eyes.

"Morning," she said, studying him.

"Morning," he replied, then hesitated. "You think Grace will be in later?"

Maggie's lips curved into the faintest smile. "She always is."

⁂

That same afternoon, Grace's phone buzzed.

"Liz," she answered, her voice soft.

"Hey, you," came her best friend's familiar warmth. "You sound like someone with too much on her heart and not enough coffee in her cup."

Grace laughed faintly. "You're not wrong. I . . . I got a job offer. Back in Ontario."

There was a pause on the line. "And?"

Grace took a deep breath. "And I don't know if that's still the life I want."

Liz's voice softened. "You've changed, Gracie. You left to find peace, not to prove something. Maybe the question isn't where you're supposed to be but who God's asking you to become there."

Grace went quiet, eyes drifting to the window where the tide was rolling in. "And then there's Glenn. He makes me feel like I can breathe again. But it's so complicated."

"Most good things are," Liz said gently. "Just make sure it's *God* leading you, not fear. And don't let the past keep you from stepping into what's next."

Grace smiled through her tears. "I know. Thanks for listening."

"I've watched you listen to everyone else for years. Now it's your turn."

⁂

That night, Glenn sat at his kitchen table. He whispered, "Lord, help me be the man I know you made me to be—steady, patient, and brave."

And somewhere across town, Grace whispered her own prayer.

Neither knew it yet, but their prayers were starting to sound a lot alike.

Today, I realized that faith isn't just about big, dramatic moments. Sometimes it's in the quiet—in the words of a best friend, in a cup of coffee slid across a counter, in a man choosing to show up instead of hiding behind walls.

I don't know what's ahead. I don't know if I should stay or go. But I do know that God is still writing this story, and I'm learning to trust Him with the spaces I can't see.

Maybe courage isn't about knowing the path but about taking the next step anyway. One step. And then another. And letting God guide the rest.

Chapter 29

CROSSROADS

It was a Tuesday. The kind of grey-sky day where the world felt wrapped in a wool blanket—soft, still, and expectant.

Grace had just finished her prep for the morning when the bell above the door jingled. She looked up, surprised to see Glenn standing there, damp from the mist and holding two travel mugs.

For a moment, neither of them spoke. The last time they'd talked, he'd told her to take care of herself—words that had felt like an ending.

He slid one mug across the counter. "Peace offering," he said.

She blinked. "You bring *me* coffee now?"

A small smile tugged at his mouth. "Don't get used to it. It's just . . . decent. I figured I owed you after our last conversation."

Grace studied him. Something in his face was different—steadier, maybe.

"You're forgiven," she said softly. "Mostly."

They stood in a familiar silence before he cleared his throat. "You busy after close?"

She hesitated. "Not really. Why?"

"There's a spot down by the old ferry line. Haven't been there in a while, but I thought maybe you'd like to see it."

Her brows lifted slightly. "Just see it?"

He shrugged. "And maybe talk. Or not. Up to you."

Grace felt a quiet surprise bloom into warmth. "Sure. I'd like that."

⁂

They drove in Glenn's old pickup, windows cracked just enough for the salty air to slip in. The ferry dock was long abandoned, its rusted ramp pulled up, the shack beside it leaning toward the ocean as if listening. But the view was clear—wide water under a slate-blue sky, restless and steady all at once.

They stood side by side, thermoses in hand, not needing to fill the air with conversation.

After a while, Glenn spoke. "This is another place I used to come to think. Or not think. Depending on the day."

Grace nodded. "Feels like a place where you can let things breathe."

He looked out at the horizon. "I didn't bring you here for anything dramatic. I just . . . wanted to share something that mattered to me."

She smiled softly. "That means a lot."

He was quiet, then said, "Claire stopped by yesterday."

Grace's fingers tightened slightly around her cup. "Oh?"

"She said she's thinking about moving back. Asked again if we could talk." He paused, his jaw working. "But the truth is, Grace, there's nothing to talk about. That part of my life's over. I just hadn't said it out loud until now."

Grace turned to him, the wind tugging at her hair. "That couldn't have been easy."

He met her gaze—steady. "No. But I'm done standing still because I'm afraid of what might break. I want to move toward what feels right."

The words hung there between them, quiet and heavy as the tide.

Grace's heart beat faster. "And you know what that is?"

He nodded once. "I think so."

They lingered there, the air sharp with salt and something new—possibility, maybe.

That night, after tidying up her kitchen, Grace settled onto the couch with a cup of tea and called Liz.

"So," Liz said, her voice sounding bright through the line. "You sound like a woman with something on her mind."

Grace smiled faintly. "You could say that. Glenn took me out to the old ferry dock today."

Liz whistled. "That sounds like a date."

"It wasn't, not exactly. But. . . ." Grace hesitated. "His ex, Claire, is back. And I got that job offer from Ontario."

"Ah," Liz said softly. "The two crossroads of the heart—what was and what could be."

Grace leaned against the counter, tracing the edge of a dish towel. "I keep thinking about what Maggie said. That love doesn't have to be loud to be real. But I don't want to mistake comfort for calling."

"Maybe it's not one or the other," Liz said. "Maybe God's giving you a chance to see what peace looks like—and what courage feels like. You'll know which one you can't live without."

Grace closed her eyes. "That's the thing. I think I already do."

He brought me coffee.

He brought me to the edge of something quiet and unfinished and said, "This matters to me."

Sometimes healing looks like choosing forward. Sometimes love is less about what's safe and more about what's true.

One good step at a time. Maybe that's all faith really is.

Chapter 30

THE SOUND OF SETTLING

The diner was quiet the rest of the week, the last of the evening light on Friday stretched across the floors in long golden lines. Grace had just locked up when her phone buzzed in her pocket—*Liz.*

She smiled, answering as she slid into the booth by the front window.

"Well, if it isn't the one person I'd trust to run this town better than the mayor," Liz teased, her voice bright through the speaker.

Grace laughed. "I think the mayor might actually be the diner."

"Probably true. How are you feeling after having a few days to think?"

Grace rested her chin in her hand. "Do you remember when I first came out here? How lost I felt?"

"I remember," Liz said softly.

"And now. . . ." Grace looked around the dimly lit diner. "I find myself memorizing the way the light hits the counter at sunset. I know the regulars by name. I've started baking again. I even organized the back pantry. Who does that unless they're planning to stay a while?"

There was a smile in Liz's voice when she said, "You're settling in."

Grace didn't deny it. "I think I am."

"Have you turned down the Ontario job then?" Liz inquired.

"No, but I think I'm going to call in the morning to let her know."

"And Glenn?"

Grace hesitated. "He's healing. Slowly. But I'm not rushing him. I just . . . want to keep walking beside him. However long he needs."

Liz was quiet for a moment. Then, gently, "You've always been good at helping people find their way. Maybe Harbor's End wasn't just about you healing—maybe it's about the people you're meant to help heal too."

Grace felt tears prick her eyes. "That sounds like something I should write down."

"You probably will," Liz said with a laugh. "Just promise me one thing?"

"What's that?"

"That you won't talk yourself out of staying if your heart's already decided to stay."

Grace curled up on the couch with her journal, the lamp casting a warm halo of light around her.

Liz asked if my heart's landed. I think it has. Not because everything's easy or clear, but because I don't feel the need to run anymore. This town, this rhythm, this gentle way of healing . . . it's enough.

I used to think home was a place. Maybe it's actually a state of peace.

And I think I'm finally there.

Chapter 31

A STEP FORWARD

The next morning, Grace woke before the sun. The house was still, the kind of still that settles in after a long wrestle of the heart. She sat at the kitchen table with a mug of tea, watching the steam rise and dissipate in the cool air. Outside, the world had turned soft and pale—a light snow dusting the rooftops, the streetlamps haloed in white.

She rehearsed what she would say a few times, though the words had already settled somewhere deep and certain. When the clock struck eight, she dialed the number.

"Carol," she began, her voice steady but warm, "thank you for the offer. Truly. But I've decided not to take the position."

There was a pause, polite and understanding, and when Grace hung up, the silence that followed didn't feel empty. It felt . . . peaceful.

She wasn't running anymore.

Before the certainty could waver, she opened her laptop and sent a message to a realtor back in Ontario: *I'd like to list the house.*

Her fingers hovered over the keyboard for a moment before she hit *send*. Then she sat back and watched the snow drift past the window, flakes tumbling and vanishing as they touched the glass.

From the direction of the wharf came the low groan of a fishing boat engine starting up—a reminder that life kept moving, tides kept turning. The sound folded over the town like a benediction, low and familiar.

Grace smiled. It was a crisp Saturday morning, and for the first time in a long while, she wasn't looking back.

⁂

The next morning, Grace found a note scribbled on the back of a faded seed catalog and tucked beside her coffee mug at the counter.

> *There's a market in Middleton on Wednesday. Thought you might like it. I'll drive. No pressure. —G*

Grace smiled when she read it. Not because it was poetic, but because it was Glenn's version of brave.

⁂

Wednesday morning came grey and soft, the kind of overcast that made colors in the trees and vendor tents seem more vivid by contrast. Glenn arrived exactly on time, truck washed, collar a little straighter than usual.

"I hear the pies there rival ours," he said as Grace climbed in.

"We'll just have to see about that."

The drive was quiet but not awkward. The kind of silence that holds space rather than fills it. Christmas music was now a staple on most of the radio stations.

At the market, they wandered past crates of apples, piles of pumpkins, and jars of homemade jam. Glenn lingered at a stand selling hand-carved bowls, quietly asking the vendor about types of wood. Grace found herself noticing the way his face softened when he talked about things he understood—tools, craftsmanship, the texture of cedar.

At one point, he handed her a paper cone of roasted cinnamon almonds.

"For your sweet tooth," he said. "Not that I've noticed or anything."

She laughed. "Very subtle."

They walked a while longer, then sat on a bench under a maple tree near the edge of the vendor stalls. Glenn shifted slightly, like something unsaid had been pressing on him the whole time.

"I never thought I'd be doing something like this again," he said quietly.

"Going to markets?" Grace asked, gently teasing.

He shook his head. "Letting someone in. Even a little."

Grace didn't push. She just waited.

Glenn continued, voice low but steady. "I used to think love was mostly about duty. Expectations. Keeping the peace. And when all that fell apart, I didn't know what was left."

He turned to look at her then.

"But lately, I've started to think maybe love is also about rest. About trust. About not needing to explain everything to be understood."

Grace held his gaze. "It can be."

A small silence settled between them, but it didn't feel like the end of a sentence. It felt like a door gently opening.

Glenn cleared his throat and stood. "There are still more stalls. I promised my mom I'd find her some of that blueberry chutney she likes."

Grace stood beside him, her smile warm. "Then let's go find it."

He handed me almonds and an invitation. Both were unexpected. Both were kind.

Glenn's not a man of many words, but today he gave me one of the rarest things we can offer someone: honesty without defense.

Sometimes healing doesn't show up as a breakthrough. Sometimes it arrives quietly, in cinnamon-scented stalls and the space to just be.

I think we're learning how to walk together. Not in leaps. But in steps.

Chapter 32

UNFOLDING

The diner was quieter than usual the following Friday morning, though the air hummed with the scent of cinnamon rolls and the low chatter of two regulars by the window. Grace moved between tables with an ease she hadn't known a few months ago. There was a rhythm to the place now—her rhythm—and she felt it deep in her chest.

Maggie watched her from the counter, wiping her hands on a towel. "You've been working on that craft show idea of yours?"

Grace smiled. "Almost ready. We've got about twenty vendors signed up now—most from town, a few from surrounding places. Mrs. Cavanaugh from the church is bringing her knitted scarves, and the youth group's making apple butter to sell. Glenn helped me convince the bakery to donate pastries for the morning crowd."

Maggie nodded approvingly. "That's no small thing, Grace. You've managed to bring half the town together without even trying."

Grace laughed softly. "I guess it just felt . . . needed. Something lighthearted. Something that reminds people we're connected." She hesitated, then added, "The church offered to host it in their hall. I thought that might make it feel more like community than commerce."

"Smart thinking," Maggie said. "You're good at that. Building bridges without making a fuss about it."

Grace turned back to the counter, aligning a stack of plates just to have something to do with her hands. "You remember that call I got from back home?"

Maggie looked up. "The one about the job?"

Grace nodded. "I called them. Told them I wouldn't be coming back."

For a moment, the clatter and hum of the diner faded beneath the weight of those words. Maggie set down her towel.

"That took courage," she said quietly.

Grace exhaled, as if finally releasing something she'd been holding too long. "It's strange. For years, I thought success was about moving up—more responsibility, bigger opportunities. But standing here, watching people laugh over pie and coffee . . . this feels more like purpose than anything I've done in a long time."

Maggie's eyes softened. "Purpose doesn't always announce itself with fanfare. Sometimes it shows up as a Friday morning with flour on your apron and peace in your heart."

Grace smiled. "Maybe so."

Maggie leaned a little closer. "Have you told Glenn yet?"

Grace shook her head. "Not yet. I want to tell him, but—"

"You're afraid he'll think it's about him," Maggie finished gently.

Grace nodded. "It's not. Not entirely, anyway."

Maggie smiled knowingly. "He'll understand. You're both learning how to let something grow without crowding it. That's rare."

The church hall smelled of cinnamon, pine, and fresh coffee—that particular mix of comfort and nerves that came with small-town events. Tables were dressed in gingham cloths, jars of preserves and handmade soaps lining the edges. Grace had been up since dawn, her apron dusted with flour from helping Maggie bake one last batch of blueberry scones.

The place was alive—laughter, chatter, the soft hum of belonging.

Glenn had come early, carrying in boxes of carved ornaments and small wooden picture frames. His hands were rough and steady, his quiet presence grounding her as always.

"Looks good," he said, surveying the rows of vendors. "You pulled this off."

Grace smiled. "*We* pulled this off."

He gave her that look, the one that always said more than words. "I'm proud of you, Grace."

She was about to reply when the door opened.

Claire stepped inside.

Even the air seemed to pause. She was polished as ever—long camel coat, sleek hair, a smile that was almost too bright for the small hall. Heads turned, whispers flickered. Grace felt her pulse steady itself out of sheer will.

Claire smiled brightly, scanning the tables before her eyes landed on Glenn. She crossed the floor, her heels clicking against the wood.

"Glenn," Claire called softly, as if no one else were there.

He turned, surprise flickering across his face. "Claire."

"You didn't call me back," she said, voice low but taut with meaning.

"I didn't have anything else to say."

Her eyes darted briefly to Grace, then back to him. "Well, we still need to talk."

She tugged at his arm, pulling him away, but still within earshot.

"I just thought . . . maybe we could try again. After everything, after what we were."

He shook his head gently. "What we were was a long time ago. And I'm not that man anymore."

Something in her expression faltered. "So, this is it, then? You're staying here? With her?"

Grace stood still, hands clasped, not stepping in but not retreating either. There was no anger in her, just quiet knowing.

Glenn's answer was simple. "Yes."

For a moment, the hum of the hall faded—just the sound of wind blowing snow around outside the windows and the faint clink of a spoon in a coffee cup nearby was all that could be heard.

Claire exhaled, her composure cracking only slightly. "Well," she said, forcing a small laugh. "Guess there's nothing left to say."

She turned, smoothing her coat as she left. The door closed behind her with a soft finality—not a slam, just an ending.

Glenn stood there for a moment, then turned to Grace. "I'm sorry."

She shook her head. "Don't be. You said what needed saying."

He nodded slowly. "I just . . . needed to be sure."

Grace smiled faintly. "Sometimes it takes seeing the past up close to know it doesn't fit anymore."

He let out a quiet breath—part relief, part release. "Yeah," he said. "It doesn't. Never really did."

The chatter of the hall rose again, life filling back in where tension had been.

"You've done a beautiful job," a woman from the church said, arranging her painted ornaments.

Grace smiled. "It's everyone's doing. I just made a few calls."

"Still," the woman said, "it takes someone with heart to pull people together like this."

Maggie bustled over with two mugs of cider, setting them down between them.

"Now," she said with a wink, "someone better buy those scones before I eat them all myself."

Grace and Glenn exchanged a look, a small smile passing between them—not dramatic, but real. The kind that meant things had settled where they were meant to.

Today I learned that closure doesn't always come with anger or tears. Sometimes it comes softly—with a door closing, a choice made, and peace that finally feels earned.

Claire came today. For a moment, the air in the hall went still—like the past had stepped right into the present, demanding attention. But Glenn stood firm. Not harshly. Just sure. And that was enough.

Watching him, I realized something: healing doesn't always mean forgetting. Sometimes it means remembering without reopening the wound.

I think that's what love really looks like—not perfection, but presence. Not grand gestures, but steady ones.

The scones sold out, the laughter lingered, and by the end of the day, the air smelled like pine, cinnamon, and grace. And for the first time in a long time, I didn't wonder what was next. I just gave thanks for now.

Chapter 33

THE TRAIL BY THE LAKE

The path was mostly quiet early Sunday afternoon, save for the crunch of snow underfoot and the occasional cry of a gull overhead. The water shimmered in the afternoon sun, its icy edges broken now and then by the slow waves.

Grace walked alongside Glenn, their strides unhurried. The trail curved gently through birches and spruce, opening every so often to glimpses of water.

"I used to come here as a kid," Glenn said. "Before the world got complicated."

Grace glanced at him. "Funny how places stay simple, even when people don't."

He nodded, eyes ahead. "I used to skip rocks from that bend over there. Told myself if I got five skips, I'd have a good day. Four skips meant it'd be okay. Three or less? I'd brace for trouble."

Grace smiled softly. "And did it work?"

"Not really," he said, chuckling under his breath. "But it gave me something to hope for."

They paused at a clearing with a fallen log near the water's edge. Glenn sat first, brushing the snow off a patch of bark with the side of his hand. Grace joined him, hands folded in her lap.

After a moment, he said, "The hardest part of starting over isn't being alone. It's knowing people are watching, waiting to see if you fail."

Grace looked at him. "I'm not waiting for that."

"I know." He paused. "That's why I keep showing up."

She didn't say anything at first. Just let the wind move around them like a quiet companion.

Then Glenn reached down and picked up a flat stone. He rubbed it between his fingers before standing up and tossing it across the surface. Four skips.

"Solid day," he said.

Grace smiled. "What's five mean these days?"

He considered. "Hope, maybe."

Another pause.

"You give me that, you know," he added as he sat back down beside her.

Grace turned toward him, surprised.

The wind moved around them like a quiet companion.

Grace drew in a slow breath. "Glenn . . . there's something I should tell you."

He turned to her, brows slightly furrowed, a little concerned about what her next words might mean.

"I called the woman from Maple Grove in Ontario yesterday," she said.

Glenn held his breath.

"Told her I wouldn't be taking the job in Ontario." She watched the water glint in the light. "And I spoke to a realtor about listing the house back home."

For a moment, all he did was stare at her—not with surprise exactly, but with the kind of stillness that comes when something inside you settles into place.

"So you're staying," he said quietly.

Grace nodded. "I'm staying."

A smile flickered across his face—small, unpolished, real. He reached for a smooth stone beside the log, weighed it in his palm, and stood.

"Then I guess that changes everything."

He threw the rock, sending it skipping across the surface—one, two, three, four, five—before it disappeared beneath the ripples.

He turned back to her, grinning fully. "Five skips," he said. "Guess it's going to be a good day."

Grace felt the truth of it settle in her chest—light and steady, like faith rediscovered.

"I don't want to rush anything," he said quickly. "But I just . . . I want to keep showing up. If that's okay."

Grace nodded slowly. "Starting with one step, right? And the next follows."

They sat watching the sun inch lower on the water. For a long time, neither spoke. There was no need to.

Today felt like a turning point, though no big words were said. Just one more step down a quiet trail beside someone willing to be seen.

There's something sacred about slow things. Not everything has to be earned in a rush. Maybe God is reminding me that trust is like a shoreline—it takes shape slowly, with every wave.

And love, when it's real, doesn't demand. It shows up. Again and again.

Chapter 34

WHEN THE QUESTIONS COME

Grace sat on the edge of the bed, her phone pressed between her shoulder and ear, a mug of tea cooling on the nightstand. Outside, the wind danced through the trees and the snow was starting to accumulate. Inside, her thoughts swirled even faster.

"Okay," Liz said through the line, "you're breathing like someone trying not to cry or scream. What's going on?"

Grace exhaled a short laugh. "Is it that obvious?"

"I've known you since before either of us had wrinkles. Spill."

Grace shifted, drawing her knees up. "Do you ever wonder if you're making something up in your head? Like, maybe I've been imagining a connection that isn't really there. Maybe it's just the newness of it all—the place, the people, the fact that someone sees me again."

"Ah," Liz said. "We've reached the Glenn portion of the call."

Grace groaned. "He's kind. Thoughtful. But quiet and guarded. And younger."

"By how much?"

"Almost ten years."

Liz paused. "Grace, I say this in love: you are *not* eighty."

"But I'm also not twenty-five. Or thirty-five. Or even forty-five."

"Good," Liz said. "Because you're not a girl anymore. You're a woman. You've lived. And if you're asking the question, *Is this real?*, then let's also ask the other: *Is it good?*"

Grace didn't answer right away.

Liz continued, softer now. "Is he respectful? Honest? Do you feel safe with him?"

"Yes," Grace said. "But it still feels so strange. Sometimes I wonder if I'm betraying Michael's memory. Like I'm moving on too quickly. Like maybe this whole second act idea is just . . . foolish."

There was silence on the other end, the kind that only a supportive best friend can insert in a conversation right before snapping you out of a funk.

"Grace," Liz said gently, "you're not betraying Michael. You're honoring the life you still have."

Grace blinked against the tears pricking her eyes.

"You loved him," Liz continued. "But that chapter closed. Not because you were done loving him but because his story here ended. Yours didn't."

A few quiet breaths passed before Grace whispered, "What if I don't even know what I want for my life anymore?"

"Then that's where you start," Liz said. "Not with Glenn. Not with anyone. With you. Ask God to show you. Ask Him if He's calling you into this. And if He is . . . trust He'll equip you."

Grace closed her eyes.

"I want to want the right things," she murmured.

"You're not chasing a fantasy, Grace," Liz said. "You're answering an invitation."

I thought I needed answers. But maybe I just needed space to ask the questions.

Liz reminded me tonight that faith doesn't always look like certainty. Sometimes it just means staying open.

I'm not done healing. But I'm also not done hoping. Maybe it's okay to be both.

Chapter 35

A CRACK IN THE ROUTINE

The morning started like any other.

Grace arrived just after sunrise, the diner still wrapped in its early hush. She unlocked the door, turned on the lights, and set a fresh pot of coffee to brew. The smell filled the air—warm, comforting, familiar.

But Maggie didn't come through the back door at her usual time.

Grace wasn't worried at first. Sometimes Maggie liked to sleep in or run a quick errand. But when twenty minutes passed, then thirty, her gut told her something was off.

She was just about to call when her phone buzzed—*Maggie*.

"Hey," came the voice on the other end—thinner than usual, a little breathy. "Don't panic, but I'm at the clinic. Doc says it's probably a drop in blood pressure. I blacked out in the kitchen this morning. Scared myself more than anything."

Grace's voice caught. "Are you okay?"

"They're doing some tests. I'll be fine. But I need you to open the diner today—if you're up for it."

"I've got it," Grace said, already grabbing an apron. "Don't worry about a thing."

"Remind Glenn I said no fuss," Maggie added before hanging up. "He'll panic if you let him."

***

The lunch rush was a blur—familiar faces, usual orders, but more questions than usual.

"Where's Maggie today?"

"She okay?"

"Tell her the town misses her."

Grace smiled through it all, but her chest stayed tight.

***

Mid-afternoon, just as things slowed, the bell above the door jingled. Glenn stepped in, his gaze scanning the place like he was expecting smoke.

"She called me," he said, approaching the counter. "Told me not to make a big deal."

"I think that was meant for both of us," Grace said, offering him a tired smile.

He didn't sit down. Just leaned against the counter, watching her hands move as she refilled pepper shakers.

"You need help?"

She blinked. "With what?"

He shrugged. "Whatever you're not asking for help with."

Grace hesitated. "I could use someone to slice pie and keep the coffee fresh."

He gave a quiet nod and headed for the back.

Later, as Grace wiped down the last table, Glenn emerged from the kitchen, drying his hands on a towel.

"She's gonna be fine," he said. "I called the clinic. They're keeping her overnight to be safe."

Grace nodded, relief washing over her.

Glenn lingered. "You held the place together today."

"I remembered how it felt when she let me help," Grace said. "Just returning the favor."

He looked at her then, something quieter in his expression. Respect, maybe. Or gratitude wrapped in something gentler.

"You didn't have to do this," he said.

"But I wanted to," Grace replied. "Sometimes the place that needs you is the one you're already in."

He didn't answer, but the silence wasn't stiff this time. It was a resting place.

I didn't expect the day to unravel. But somehow, in the uncertainty, we all moved closer.

God doesn't always shake foundations. Sometimes He just nudges things out of place—enough to make us look around and notice what we've built together.

Today reminded me that service isn't something we give after we have it all figured out. It's what shapes us as we walk.

Chapter 36

A LIGHT LEFT ON

The diner was quieter than usual the next day. The regulars had filtered out, and only a few dishes clinked softly in the sink.

Grace stood by the window, watching the last of the light sink below the horizon. Glenn had stayed behind to help close. Neither of them said much.

Finally, he broke the silence.

"She was the only steady thing after everything went sideways," he said, not looking at her. "After my ex . . . after the divorce. Maggie—well, Mom—just . . . kept showing up."

Grace turned toward him slowly. "She's always been that for you."

He nodded. "Even when I didn't deserve it. Even when I shut her out."

There was a long pause.

"I don't know what I'd do if something happened to her," he added, the words barely above a whisper. "It's like I only just got her back after years of pretending I was fine."

Grace didn't speak right away. She took a few steps closer but kept a respectful distance. "Do you want me to pray with you?"

He looked at her—surprised, maybe. Or uncertain.

Then, finally, he nodded once.

They stood there, not touching, not needing to. Grace bowed her head.

"God," she said softly, "You know what's unspoken in this room. Thank You for Maggie. For her faithfulness. For her presence. Give her rest. Give Glenn peace. Let him feel Your steadiness, even now." Her voice faltered just slightly, then steadied again. "And thank You that we don't have to hold all of this alone."

When she finished, Glenn exhaled like he'd been holding his breath for years.

"Thanks," he said, voice gruff. "For that."

She gave a small nod. "Anytime."

They didn't say much else as they finished up. But as Glenn stepped out into the night, he paused and looked back.

"You're good at that, you know," he said.

"At what?"

"Making things feel less . . . heavy."

Grace smiled softly. "Maybe I've just had some experience learning that we're not meant to carry it all."

He nodded, then walked into the dark, headlights flicking on as he pulled out into the quiet street.

And Grace stood for a moment longer, watching, before locking the door behind her.

He let me pray with him. I didn't expect that. Didn't ask for it. But when the moment came, it was holy.

There's something tender about trusting someone enough to say nothing fancy. Just, "God, we need You."

Grief changes us. And gratitude humbles us. Glenn's heart may be quiet, but it's beating toward something. I think I saw that tonight.

Chapter 37

WHEN JOY RETURNS

The diner buzzed with its usual morning rhythm—coffee cups clinking, the low hum of conversation, Maggie calling out an order to the back.

Grace stood by table four, refilling Mr. Hatfield's coffee when something across the street caught her eye. A truck door opened. A familiar figure stepped out, backlit by the rising sun.

Jonas.

She froze mid-pour, her eyes wide, heart leaping. Without thinking, she placed the coffee pot gently on the table and bolted for the door.

Maggie blinked from behind the counter. "Grace?"

But Grace didn't answer. She pushed open the diner's door, the bell jingling behind her as she darted across the road.

Jonas turned at the sound of her footsteps. His face broke into a wide grin.

"Well, I'll be—" he started.

Grace threw her arms around him before he could finish, and he caught her in a laughter-filled hug, spinning her once for good measure.

"You're really here!" she said, breathless.

"Of course I am. Harbor's End doesn't let go that easy," he chuckled.

When they pulled back, Grace finally noticed the woman rounding the front of the truck—a gentle smile on her face, dark curls pulled back in a loose bun, eyes full of quiet warmth.

"Oh," Grace said softly, eyes shifting to Jonas with delighted realization.

"This is Leah," Jonas said, pride and peace in his voice. "We met through the church plant. Grace Templeton, meet the woman I prayed I'd never be too old to find."

Leah laughed lightly. "He talks about you all the time."

That made Grace laugh too—the full-hearted, happy kind that filled the street.

"Well then," Grace said, without hesitation, pulling Leah into a warm embrace. "Welcome to Harbor's End."

Maggie stood in the diner window, watching with a soft smile as the three made their way back across the street. She shook her head once—not in disbelief, but in something like awe.

Back inside, Jonas slid into his usual seat at the counter. It felt like no time had passed at all.

"Same old coffee?" Grace asked with a grin.

"You better believe it."

Leah sat beside him, her hands wrapped around a tea mug. She was gentle-spoken but full of quiet strength—the kind that Grace instantly respected.

As the morning rolled on, they laughed, caught up, and shared stories. Leah asked questions about the town, and Grace found herself answering like someone who'd lived there for decades. At one point, Maggie came out from the kitchen, wiped her hands on her apron, and just hugged Jonas without a word.

The whole diner seemed to breathe differently that day—lighter, warmer.

Grace watched the two of them—Jonas and Leah—and felt no ache, only gratitude. This wasn't a goodbye. It was a new chapter for them, and for her.

God was still writing.

He came back—not to stay, but for the holidays and to remind me that faith is movement, not stillness.

Jonas has found joy again. And not because he chased it, but because he followed God's voice. Leah carries peace like a lantern. No wonder they found each other.

Today was a reminder: nothing's lost when we keep our hands open. Love returns in all kinds of ways. Sometimes with a laugh, sometimes with a hug on a sidewalk, and sometimes with tea and pie and stories shared like family.

Chapter 38

ECHOES

Glenn hadn't stayed long that morning.

He'd come in just after the breakfast rush, as usual. But when he saw Jonas at the counter, laughing beside Grace and a woman he didn't recognize, something in him paused. He hesitated by the door, fingers brushing the brim of his ball cap, then quietly turned and left without a word.

Grace noticed. She didn't chase him.

That afternoon, the diner felt too quiet without Jonas's laugh. Maggie had slipped out early to rest, and Leah had gone for a walk to see the shoreline. Grace wiped the counters, her movements slow and thoughtful.

The bell above the door jingled.

Glenn stepped in, his boots softer than usual on the worn tile floor. He didn't go to his usual booth. Instead, he walked to the counter and took the stool beside Grace.

"Coffee?" she asked, voice light.

He nodded. "Please."

She poured without speaking, sliding the mug toward him.

"I saw him," Glenn said finally, eyes on the swirl of cream in his cup. "Across the street this morning."

Grace nodded. "He was excited to come back. Wanted us to meet Leah."

"She seems . . . good," Glenn said after a moment. "Solid. Kind."

"She is."

He took a sip, then set the mug down carefully. "Funny, isn't it? How some people move forward like it's nothing. Like it's easy."

Grace leaned on the counter, arms folded gently. "I don't think it's ever easy. But I think for some, the timing lines up with the healing. For others . . . the healing comes more slowly."

He looked at her. "And for others still?"

"They're still deciding if it's worth trying."

That sat between them for a while.

Glenn rubbed a hand across his jaw. "He's lucky," he said quietly. "To have loved . . . and then loved again."

Grace hesitated. "You still believe that's possible?" Trying to read his expression.

Glenn didn't answer. He just looked down at the worn grooves in the counter, the mug warming his hands.

Grace didn't push. She just offered a small, quiet smile. "Coffee's on the house today."

Glenn gave a half-smile—the first in days. "Thanks."

He stayed a while longer than usual, not saying much, but not rushing off either.

Sometimes healing continues in silence, in shared space, and in one person staying put long enough for the other to feel safe.

Not all change comes with fanfare. Sometimes it's a man who usually runs staying seated. Sometimes it's a half-smile from someone who hasn't looked you in the eye for days.

I used to think growth had to be dramatic. Now I see that it often looks like ordinary days and second cups of coffee.

Glenn is wrestling. But he's still here. And maybe that's enough for today.

Chapter 39

THE PUSH

The diner had closed early Christmas Eve. One of those slow days as people are out and about making last-minute preparations.

Maggie said she would lock up, so Grace headed home early.

Glenn stayed behind to restock the coffee supplies. He moved in silence, stacking boxes beneath the counter, half lost in thought.

"You've been brooding," Maggie said from the doorway, leaning on the frame.

He didn't turn around. "I've been thinking."

"Well," she said dryly, "maybe it's time you stopped thinking and started doing."

That made him pause.

Maggie came in slowly, eased herself onto a stool, and let out a long breath. "I've watched you walk around like a ghost for years, Glenn. Quiet, careful, shut down. And I didn't push. You needed space. Time. I get it."

She folded her hands on the counter.

"But something's changed."

Glenn finally turned to face her. "Changed how?"

"You," she said. "Since Grace showed up. You come in more. You stay longer. You don't bark at the regulars like you used to."

He gave a slight smirk.

Maggie leaned forward. "You care, Glenn. And don't act like you don't. You care about her."

He didn't deny it.

"I'm not saying you need to marry her tomorrow," Maggie said. "But I am saying this: if you keep waiting for the perfect moment, if you keep letting the past tell you what the future's allowed to be, you're going to wake up one day and realize you missed it."

Glenn looked down. "It's not that simple."

"No, it's not. It's hard and scary and messy," she said. "But you don't get love without risk. You don't get healing without trust. And at some point, Son, you've got to pee or get off the pot."

That made him bark out a laugh—short and surprised.

"I mean it," she added, more gently now. "You think Grace is going to wait around forever for you to decide if you're going to trust her or not? She's not chasing you, Glenn. But she is waiting—in her own quiet way. And you need to decide if you're going to meet her halfway."

He sat down beside her, elbows on the counter, silent for a long time.

"What if I mess it up?" he finally asked.

"You might," Maggie said without hesitation. "But what if you don't? What if it's the one good thing God's trying to give back to you?"

Another beat of silence.

Then Maggie stood slowly and kissed the top of his head.

"Don't let fear win twice," she whispered.

And with that, she left him alone in the diner, the scent of coffee and lemon cleaner filling the space around him.

Glenn prayed, *God, I don't know what to do with a love that's gentle. One that doesn't force or threaten or twist my insides. But maybe . . . maybe that's the kind I need. And maybe she's the one You've been preparing me for—not to rescue me, but to stand beside me as I finally step out of the shadow.*

A verse he had memorized as a child suddenly came to mind: "Trust in the Lord with all your heart, and lean not on your own understanding; in all your ways acknowledge Him and He will make your paths straight."

"Proverbs 3:5-6," Glenn recalled aloud. "Hmm."

Chapter 40

A CLEAR PATH

Glenn stood on the porch of the rental house later Christmas morning, one hand in his pocket, the other holding a small paper bag from the general store. The morning was crisp, but the sun was shining, making the blanket of snow glisten like millions of crystals.

He didn't knock right away.

He'd thought about this all night—prayed about it, even. Not for a sign. Not for a perfect outcome. Just for the courage to stop waiting for one.

Finally, he knocked—twice, steady.

Grace opened the door, a dish towel still in her hands. Her hair was loosely tied back, her expression surprised but soft.

"Glenn," she said, stepping aside.

He came in, removing his boots at the door. The paper bag crinkled quietly in his hand.

"I brought you something," he said, holding it out. "Merry Christmas."

She took it with a curious glance and peeked inside. A simple wooden cross lay nestled in tissue. Rough-edged but beautiful, clearly hand-carved.

"I made it yesterday," he said. "After I left the diner."

"Glenn—" she began, but he gently interrupted.

"I need to say something. And I want to say it before I talk myself out of it."

She gave a small nod and set the cross on the table.

He took a breath. "I've spent a lot of time hiding. From people, from truth, from God. And I think somewhere along the line, I decided that I didn't deserve anything good. That love was for other people. Faith was for those who didn't mess everything up."

He met her eyes then—fully, squarely.

"But I was wrong. God's been patient with me. And you. . . ." He swallowed. "You've shown up in ways that made it hard to keep hiding."

He stepped forward slightly, giving her space to step back if she needed. She didn't.

"I'm not perfect," he said. "You already know that. But I'm growing. And I want to lead—not just in work or faith but in how I love others. If God's giving me another chance at something good, I don't want to miss it."

Grace's eyes brimmed with tears, but her smile was steady.

"I'm not asking for an answer today," he added quickly. "I just needed you to know I see what's here. And I'd like to pursue it—carefully, prayerfully. If that's something you're open to."

Grace stepped forward then, her hand brushing gently against his arm.

"I am," she said quietly. "But I need to know we're walking in step with God, not just each other."

"We will," he promised. "That's the only way I know how to move forward now."

They stood in that quiet agreement, the cross on the table behind them—a simple symbol of the kind of love they were beginning to believe in.

He came to the door. Not just to visit. But to speak. To lead.

There's a strength in him I hadn't seen before—not the kind that fights battles with fists, but the kind that shows up with a carving and a prayer and a heart that's being made new.

I don't know what the next chapter holds, but I think this is how it begins: with clarity, with courage, and with God at the centre.

Chapter 41

TEA AND TRUTH

The kettle whistled in Grace's quiet kitchen, a comforting sound that pulled her from the swirl of thoughts she hadn't yet pinned down. She poured the water over her tea bag—chamomile, for calm—and took her mug to the couch where her phone waited, already on speaker.

"Still with me, Liz?" Grace asked as she settled in.

"Always," came the warm voice on the other end. "I've got my Earl Grey steeping. Now spill."

Grace let out a half-laugh, half-sigh. "He came over this morning."

There was a pause. Then, "Glenn?"

"Yeah."

"Well. Don't keep me in suspense."

Grace smiled, staring at the rising steam. "He brought me a cross he carved. Simple, beautiful. Then he told me—well, not in so many words, but he basically said he wants to pursue a relationship. Intentionally. With God at the center."

Silence.

"Liz?"

"I'm just smiling so wide my face hurts," Liz said. "Grace Templeton, do you realize how long I've prayed for a moment like this?"

"It caught me off guard," Grace admitted. "He was so steady. Sure. Not pushy, just . . . present."

"That's because he's been doing the work. Quietly. Like a tree growing roots before it ever reaches for the sun."

Grace blinked at the image. "That's beautiful."

"I think it's what you needed," Liz said softly. "Not someone to sweep you off your feet, but someone who walks beside you. Slow and steady. Faith first."

Grace swallowed. "There's still a lot to figure out. I'm older. We have baggage. He's still healing. So am I."

"And yet," Liz said, "God brought you together. Not to fix each other but to point each other back to Him."

Grace didn't reply right away.

Then she said, "Do you think it's too late? To begin again like this?"

"Oh, Grace," Liz said, her voice thick with love. "God specializes in beginnings that don't make sense on paper. You're not too late. You're right on time."

Tears pricked Grace's eyes. She wiped them away before they could fall.

"I needed to hear that," she whispered.

"I know," Liz said. "And when you forget again, I'll remind you. That's what best friends—and tea—are for."

They sat in companionable silence for a few moments, sipping from different provinces but tethered by years of life, loss, and love.

"I'm proud of you," Liz added. "For opening your heart again. For letting God lead."

Grace smiled into her mug. "I think I'm just learning to follow."

Sometimes God speaks through the whispers of a friend on the other end of the line.

I don't have it all figured out. But I don't need to. Trust means walking even when you don't see the whole path.

I think this is the start of something real. Not perfect. But holy.

Chapter 42

TOGETHER, BEFORE GOD

The diner was quiet the Saturday it reopened after Christmas. The windows fogged slightly from the contrast between the evening air outside and the warmth within. Grace was wiping down the counter for the last time that night, the lights dimmed, the chairs already turned up on the tables.

Glenn stepped out from the kitchen, rubbing his hands on a towel. "All set back there," he said.

"Me too," Grace replied.

They stood there for a moment, neither in a rush to leave. Something about the silence wasn't empty—it was expectant.

"Can I ask you something?" Glenn said, walking toward the counter.

"Of course."

He looked down for a moment, then up again, eyes clear. "Would you . . . would you pray with me?"

Grace stilled. Not because she was surprised, but because her heart swelled at the question.

"Yes," she said. "I'd like that."

They moved to a small booth near the back—the one Jonas used to sit at—and slid in across from each other. Glenn reached his hands out across the table, and Grace took them gently. They bowed their heads.

He started, his voice quiet but sure.

"God . . . we don't know what the future holds. But we know You hold us. Thank You for second chances, for quiet healing, for people who don't give up on us. Thank You for Grace"—he paused, squeezing her hands lightly—"and for the way You've used her to remind me who I really am. Who You are."

Grace took a breath and added her voice.

"Lord, we give this next step to You—whatever it is. We don't want to run ahead of You, and we don't want to lag behind. Help us walk in step with Your Spirit. Keep our hearts soft. Keep our hands open. And thank You for Glenn—for his courage, his gentleness, his growth. I see Your fingerprints all over his life. In Jesus's name. Amen."

They sat in the stillness that followed.

When they opened their eyes, they didn't need to say much more.

Glenn smiled. "I think that's the most honest thing I've said in a long time."

Grace smiled back. "I think it's the beginning of something . . . *right*."

Tonight, Glenn asked me to pray with him. Not because we had to, or because something was wrong, but because something was right.

We're not rushing into anything. No declarations or big decisions. Just a shared moment, hands clasped across a table, hearts laid bare before God.

And in that moment, I realized: this is what trust looks like. Not certainty, but surrender. Not control, but presence. A willingness to let God write the next line, even if the ink is still wet from the last.

I used to think the best parts of my story were behind me. Now I see—maybe they were just the prologue.

Chapter 43

THE HANDOFF

Maggie had started sitting more. At first, it was subtle—she'd pause between refilling salt shakers or sit for a few extra minutes with a cup of tea at the corner booth. But lately, Grace noticed she no longer bothered to pretend she wasn't tired. She just was.

That morning, Grace walked in early to prep and found Maggie already there—not in the kitchen but perched on a stool behind the counter, slowly tearing open a packet of sweetener for her tea.

"You're in early," Grace said, hanging up her coat.

"Couldn't sleep," Maggie replied. "Thought I'd come in before the world got noisy."

Grace poured herself a coffee and leaned beside her. "Everything all right?"

Maggie gave a quiet smile. "More than all right, I think."

Grace raised an eyebrow.

Maggie stared into her tea for a moment before speaking. "I've been doing this a long time. Pouring coffee, listening to stories, watching the same people walk through that door at the same hour every day. I've loved it. But I think . . . I think I'm ready for the next thing."

Grace's chest tightened. "You're thinking about moving?"

"I visited that retirement place," Maggie said. "Where my friend Marlene is. It's peaceful. They play Scrabble every Thursday and complain about the pudding. I didn't hate it."

Grace let out a soft laugh. "High praise."

Maggie looked at her, her tone turning gentle. "But I couldn't consider it unless I knew this place was going to be okay. That Glenn was okay."

Grace's smile softened. "He's more than okay, Maggie. He's really coming back to life."

"That's because of you," Maggie said, her voice thickening. "I haven't seen him smile like that in years. Haven't heard him humming to himself in the kitchen since he was a boy."

Grace blinked. "He hums?"

"Terribly," Maggie said, smiling. "But it's beautiful to me."

They sat in silence for a beat before Maggie cleared her throat and reached into her coat pocket. She pulled out a small ring of keys—worn, familiar, the brass dull from years of use—and set them on the counter between them.

"What's this?" Grace asked.

"Consider it a trial," Maggie said. "You and Glenn run the place for a while. I'll still come in now and then, make sure you're not putting pickles in the apple pie. But I want to see what it's like to let go."

Grace stared at the keys. "You sure?"

"I'm not dying, Grace. Just letting God open a new door. And something tells me"—she glanced toward the back where Glenn had come in and was restocking shelves—"a new door's opening for you too."

Grace touched the keys gently. “Thank you. Truly.”

Maggie reached for her hand. “And when he asks you, don’t hesitate. God doesn’t bring love like that twice without a reason.”

Grace didn’t reply. She didn’t need to.

She handed me the keys today. Not just to a building, but to a space filled with stories, laughter, and second chances. I never imagined a place like this could feel like home—or that someone else’s legacy could become part of my own.

Maggie said it’s just a trial. But I think we both know: some trials are really just transitions disguised as opportunities.

And maybe, just maybe . . . something else beautiful is beginning.

Chapter 44

SOMETHING NEW BEGINS

The next morning, Grace unlocked the diner using the front door key Maggie had given her the day before. Until now, she'd always entered through the side door using the keypad code Maggie had shared when she first started helping out. But this? This was different. Turning a physical key in the front lock felt . . . official. Ceremonial, even.

She stood just inside the door for a long moment, the hush of the empty space wrapping around her. The booths, the counter, the familiar smell of cinnamon and coffee—it all felt the same. But she didn't.

Glenn arrived not long after. He stepped inside, pausing when he saw her behind the counter.

"You beat me here," he said.

She held up the keyring, a slight grin tugging at the corner of her mouth. "Perks of the job, apparently."

He walked to the counter, setting down a bag of fresh rolls from the bakery. "She did it, huh?"

Grace nodded. "Said she wants to try out life at the retirement home for real. Gave me the keys. Asked us to run the place together. At least for now."

Glenn leaned on the counter, silent for a moment. Then, in a low voice, he said, "She's not just trying it out, you know. She's letting go."

Grace looked at him. "Are you okay with that?"

He hesitated. "A month ago, I would've said no. Two weeks ago, I might've panicked. But now?" He gave her a quiet smile. "Now, I think it's time."

They busied themselves with the usual morning prep—coffee brewing, butter pats laid out, menus wiped down. But the air between them carried something different. Anticipation. Partnership.

As the first regulars trickled in—Mr. Delaney for his usual black coffee and toast, followed by the Robsons with their matching orders of oatmeal—Grace moved with a steadiness she hadn't felt in years. Glenn moved alongside her, not stepping ahead, not trailing behind. Just . . . in step.

Mid-morning, when things had slowed again, they found themselves alone behind the counter. Glenn glanced toward the door, then back at Grace.

"I know Maggie gave you the keys," he said, voice quieter now. "But I was wondering . . . is this something you want? Not just for now. But long term?"

Grace leaned back slightly, considering the question.

"I don't know what forever looks like," she admitted. "But this? Yes. For now, and maybe for longer."

Glenn nodded slowly. "Then maybe we let this be the start of something new."

He didn't reach for her hand. Didn't say anything that would press her too fast or too far. But the way he looked at her—steady, sure—was its own kind of promise.

Grace smiled. "Something new sounds just right."

Today felt like a beginning. Not flashy or grand—but like planting a seed in warm soil and trusting the rain will come. Maggie handed over the keys, but what she really passed on was belief. In us. In this town. In God still writing stories that matter.

I don't know exactly what the future holds. But I'm finally starting to believe it might be good. And that maybe, just maybe, I'm not walking into it alone.

Chapter 45

THE RETURN

It was a slow Wednesday morning, the kind where the clink of cutlery and hum of conversation felt more like background music than business.

Grace was refilling a sugar jar when the bell above the diner door jingled.

She glanced up—and there he was again.

Jonas and Leah, giving Grace a warm smile and a small wave.

Grace greeted them both with a hug. "You didn't say you were stopping by again."

"When you texted about Maggie handing you guys the keys, I had to see it with my own eyes," Jonas said, walking toward the counter.

Grace laughed. "Don't worry. We haven't taken your booth away."

He grinned, sliding into his place at the counter. Leah sat beside him, folding her hands around a cup Grace set down.

The place had shifted since his last visit. Maggie was gone, not just from the kitchen but from the rhythm of the place. Glenn had started helping Grace more steadily, even on weekends. There were new specials chalked on the board. A fresh coat of paint near the window. But most of all, there was a calm steadiness in Grace now that hadn't been there before.

Jonas noticed it. He could see that Glenn noticed it too, in the way he studied her when she laughed with a regular or moved with ease behind the counter.

"This feels . . . different," he said, almost wistfully. "But good."

"It's become home," Grace said quietly.

He nodded. "Leah and I are getting more involved with the church plant. Small group nights. Youth mentoring. Never thought I'd be doing that at my age."

"Never too late," Grace said with a knowing smile.

They chatted a bit longer. Before they left, Jonas rested a hand on Grace's shoulder. "You ever want to come out and see it all, just say the word. We've got space."

Grace smiled. "We'll see. But I think I know where I'm meant to be."

Jonas nodded slowly, then added with a grin, "Just don't forget to save me a slice of pie next time."

Chapter 46

THE SURPRISE

The dinner rush had been steady but not overwhelming, and by the time Grace flipped the sign to *Closed* and locked the front door, her shoulders were pleasantly tired.

Glenn was still wiping down the counter, his movements deliberate.

"Come sit," he said softly, nodding toward one of the booths near the window.

Grace raised a brow. "You're bossing me around now?"

He grinned. "Just . . . humor me."

When she slid into the booth, she noticed a small velvet box resting on the table. Her breath caught.

Glenn didn't rush. He sat across from her, folding his hands as if about to pray—which he was. "Before I say anything, I need to thank God for what He's done. For bringing you here. For not letting me stay stuck in the shadows."

His voice was low, steady. "Lord, I don't deserve her, but You've shown me that love isn't about deserving—it's about giving, trusting, and walking together in Your light. If it's Your will, let this be the beginning of something that honors You."

When he opened his eyes, Grace felt her own fill with tears. Glenn slid the box toward her and opened it. Inside was a delicate ring—simple gold with a single diamond, worn smooth with time.

"It was my grandmother's," he said. "Maggie gave it to me when she was packing this up. She said she wanted it to go to the woman who would walk beside me in faith and life."

Grace swallowed hard, blinking away the blur. "Glenn—"

"I'm not promising perfection. I'm promising to seek God first, to protect what we have, and to keep stepping out of the shadows with you at my side. Grace, will you marry me?"

Her yes came with a laugh and a tear in the same breath. Glenn slid the ring onto her finger, his hands warm and steady. They bowed their heads together, whispering a prayer of thanks, the quiet hum of the diner their only witness.

Chapter 47

ENTRUSTED

The lunch rush had tapered off, leaving the diner in that comfortable hush where the scent of coffee lingered and sunlight pooled in quiet corners. Grace was wiping down the counter when Maggie slid into her usual booth, tea in hand. Glenn joined them a moment later, carrying a plate of pie he hadn't paid for—standard practice by now.

Maggie looked at them for a long moment before speaking. "You two make a good team."

Grace smiled. "We try."

"No," Maggie said, shaking her head. "You *are* a good team. And I've been thinking . . . it's time this place had a new heartbeat. Mine's slowing down."

Glenn set his fork down. "Mom, you're talking like you've got one foot in the grave."

"I'm talking about something bigger." She leaned forward, her eyes bright but steady. "I'm selling the diner. To you two."

Grace's eyes widened. "Maggie, we can't—"

"You can. And I'm not asking for money. This place has paid me back tenfold over the years—not in dollars but in *purpose*. After your dad died," she said, glancing at Glenn, "after my husband passed, this diner kept me going. It was my love, my mission, my way to keep giving to this town. But seasons change."

Glenn's brow furrowed. "And the retirement home? You really planning to move there?" His voice was cautious, almost protective.

Maggie took a slow sip of her tea, then smiled. "When I went to stay for that trial visit and again this last time, I'll admit, I wasn't sure. But you know what? I loved it. There's a garden where the ladies meet every morning, and I've already been roped into helping with the spring planting. They say I have 'dirt under my nails energy,' whatever that means."

Her eyes twinkled. "And there's a group who meets in the evenings for trivia night. I joined them once—our team name was The Forget-Me-Nots. We came dead last, but I haven't laughed that hard in years. Oh, and Edna from across the hall bakes a peach cobbler that could put even mine to shame. Don't tell anyone I said that."

Something in Glenn's face softened. "You sound . . . happy."

"I am," Maggie said softly. "It feels like the right time. And knowing you two are here, I can make that move without worry."

Glenn hesitated, then let out a breath, the tension in his shoulders easing. "You're sure about this?"

"I want it in the hands of people who see it the way I do—not as a business but as a ministry. And that's you two."

Maggie reached across the table, taking both their hands in hers. "Run it together. Keep feeding people's stomachs and their souls. That's all I ask."

Glenn glanced at Grace, then back to his mother. A quiet smile spread over his face. "We'll take care of it. We promise."

As they closed up for the night, the neon sign flickering off in the window, Grace looked around at the empty booths and polished counter. She could almost hear the echoes of every laugh, every conversation, every prayer whispered over coffee cups.

Whatever comes next, she thought, *I'll be ready. Because now, I believe—it's never too late to become who God created us to be; to find the place we belong.*

THE NOTE FROM JONAS

For Grace.

There was a time I thought my story was winding down. Then someone reminded me—gently, consistently—that God doesn't end chapters with silence. He ends them with redemption. And sometimes, He begins new ones in places we never planned to be.

This poem came from those in-between moments. I wrote it just for you—if you're still waiting, still hoping, still wondering if God's not finished with you yet.

Keep walking. He goes ahead of you.

—Jonas

For the One Still Walking

A poem by Jonas Reid

When the silence stretches longer
Than you thought your faith could hold,
When your prayers feel unanswered
And the nights grow deep and cold—

Don't mistake the quiet waiting
For a God who's stepped away.
Sometimes love is found in stillness,
In the grace to stay.

When the road before you narrows
And the past won't let you be,
Lift your eyes toward the shoreline—
There's a Hand that parts the sea.

You are not the sum of sorrow,
You are not the ache alone.
You were made for sacred purpose,
And your heart was shaped for Home.

So take another step, beloved,
Even trembling feet will do.
He's not finished with your story—
There is more. There's more for you.

www.ingramcontent.com/pod-product-compliance
Lightning Source LLC
LaVergne TN
LVHW090611110826
845146LV00001B/336

* 9 7 9 8 8 8 9 2 8 1 6 5 8 *